Destined For The Drakari Warlords

Celestial Mates

Aurelia Skye

Published by Amourisa Press, 2021.

Join Kit's Mailing List[1] **to receive notification of new releases and access bonus chapters for your favorite books. You get free books just for signing up. If you prefer to receive notifications for just one, or a few, of Kit's pen names, you'll have the option to select which lists to subscribe to at signup.**

---

1. http://kittunstall.com/newsletter/

Blurb

Celestial Mates—Romancing the Galaxy...

ONE MOMENT, EVA IS on Earth, helping restore the destroyed planet, and the next, she's whisked to a far-off galaxy, away from her parents and the other cyborgs and humans. She arrives in the middle of a mating ceremony for the two newest rulers, Vander and Virgo. The gorgeous green men are pure temptation, especially since they seem to believe she's meant to be their mate, but Eva wants to go home. She controls her own destiny, not a blobby peach alien.

Life on Senufo is strange, and she longs for Earth...until her mates win her over, and she starts to fall in love. Is she truly stranded on Senufo as Freydon Rote, the meddling Celestial Mates agent, claims? Or is there a way back to Earth? Will she even want to find it once she surrenders to the tender seductions offered by her Drakari warlord mates?

This is a story in the Celestial Mates universe and features everyone's favorite meddlesome agent, Freydon Rote. He made a perfect match for Eva's parents, Carrie and DVS (from "Mated To The Cyborg General"), so did he get it right again for Eva, or did he make a mistake? Read to find out.

P.S. You don't need to have read the Cybernetic Hearts series to read Eva's story.

Chapter 1

VANDER MADE A CARELESS swipe to his chest to remove most of the blood oozing from the wound, giving it little thought. He could feel the pain, but it had fueled him on to victory, along with his twin brother, Virgo. It was obvious to everyone he and Virgo had been victorious. They were the only ones to complete the last set of challenges. They had won the trials, and Chief Barta was just about to announce the results formally. They would inherit the chiefdom soon. Before that, they would finally learn the identity of their mate or mates.

A hush fell over the crowd as Barta stood on the dais, lifting her arms. The amphitheater was filled with water that remained from the last challenge against the *saard* they had vanquished. "By right of trial and victory over the challenges, my successors are Vander and Virgo Skry."

Now the crowd broke its silence, cheering wildly. Vander was aware several of his fellow Drakari were excited. Vander knew that was a good sign. If there were murmurs of discontent among the crowd, the rulers taking over the chiefdom were sure to have a harder battle to be accepted.

Feltha Nip, the shaman, stepped forward then. "It's now time to perform the ceremony to find your mates."

Vander tensed with anticipation, and he could feel Virgo doing the same. They didn't look alike, but they were still twins and shared many of the same emotions and reactions.

Feltha said some words and moved her hands around in a ceremonial configuration Vander had not seen before. He'd witnessed other mating match ceremonies, but her handwork had been different. Perhaps it was because they were soon-to-be new Chiefs that she had to do something different. With a flash of green, a woman appeared in front of them.

At least he thought she was a woman. She had a pleasing feminine shape, but she was unlike anything he'd ever seen before. Where he and the rest of the Drakari had varying shades of green skin, this woman had a pale golden color. Her hair appeared to be dark brown or black, and it floated around her face in an enticing fashion as she gasped quickly, suggesting she was on the verge of panic.

"What is it?" asked a few voices behind him.

Vander couldn't explain why that put them on the defensive, but he left his position on the platform to glide to the strange creature who'd appeared among them. He knelt beside her, and Virgo appeared a second later on her other side.

"What's going on? Where am I? How am I breathing underwater?" Her eyes were wide and darting around in clear panic. She hugged herself and flinched when Vander tried to touch her shoulder. Virgo got the same response when he tried to offer comfort.

"Calm down and breathe." Vander said the words firmly, trying to get her attention and cut through her anxiety.

"How can I breathe underwater?" She asked the question again, more vehemently this time. Her hand lifted to touch her throat, where she had three discreet slits, which were gills that allowed her to breathe underwater. She looked even more terrified when she felt them. "This is impossible."

Virgo's tone was gentle. "Try to calm down so we can determine how you came to be here."

At first, she didn't seem to hear him as her vivid blue eyes continued darting around the amphitheater in the fortress, where everyone had gathered for the trials. Slowly, her gaze started to focus on Virgo as he talked slowly and gently to her. Vander was glad his twin was able to get through to her, but he couldn't help feeling annoyed that she had virtually ignored him. It was an irrational response, but he was used to listening to his emotions and instincts. He had to gnash his teeth together to keep from demanding her attention. He shook his head at the reaction, unaccustomed to being so senseless.

When she finally had calmed down enough that she could speak without that edge of hysteria, she said, "I need land."

Vander and Virgo exchanged a look of puzzlement, but they both took one of her arms and started swimming up toward the surface. They spent most of their life underwater, but they could breathe on land just as well, though it was strange to step onto solid land again each time they did so, though the fortress was usually kept free of water, except for ceremonies. The ground was rockier and felt different from the construction in the fortress, though he couldn't explain why.

She seemed to calm down even further when she was seated on one of the crystalline structures protruding from the ground. At least until she looked into the sky and saw their orange sun and the purple-green sky behind it. She started breathing heavily again, so Vander took her hand and squeezed gently. Her pale golden skin was a strange contrast to the vivid green of his, but a jolt shot through him when he touched her.

"Where am I?" Her voice was trembling, and she seemed on the edge of panic again.

"This is the planet Senufo," said Vander.

She shook her head, seeming to want to reject the information he'd offered. "How did I get here? How can this be?" Her hand went to a pendant around her neck, and she squeezed it as though it was her lifeline.

Vander gasped. "You have a Drakari mate charm."

She gave him a blank stare. "I have a what?"

He nodded toward the pendant she held in her hand. "It's given to all Drakari at birth. When it lights up, it indicates you've found your mate. How did you come to have one? You're clearly not Drakari." He felt a stirring of suspicion, though he had no justification for it.

The tribes of Senufo had been peaceful for at least the last hundred years. It was unlikely any of the tribes would try to attack in such a strange fashion, even though word had surely spread that Barta's twin had died two months ago, and so the chiefdom would be opening to a new set of twins or triplets.

She shook her head. "I don't know what you're talking about, but I've always been told this was a good luck charm. It was a gift from Freydon Rote, when I was born. Do you know Freydon?"

Vander shook his head. "I have no knowledge of that name."

Virgo reached out to stroke her hand, which clutched the pendant. She trembled slightly before her hand loosened, revealing the pendant. Virgo studied it, as did Vander, and when they looked at each other, they nodded. They were close enough that they often could communicate without words, and they both agreed this was certainly a Drakari mate charm.

"Where are you from?" asked Virgo.

"Earth." She shuddered. "We have our problems, and terraforming is taking longer than expected, but I'd rather be back on Earth right now. What is this place? And how can I breathe underwater?" As she asked the question, she fingered the gills on the side of her neck again and shuddered. "Where did they come from?"

"Your gills?" asked Vander. "You didn't have them before?"

She shook her head. "Where I'm from, I can't breathe underwater, and I certainly don't have gills. How is any of this possible?" Her eyes narrowed suddenly. "Freydon Rote, if you're behind this, show yourself."

Though she clearly wasn't addressing him, Vander waited for a moment, not sure what she was expecting with her angry demand. Whatever it was, it didn't happen. He could tell by the way her shoulders slumped, and she shook her head.

"Do you have some way to get me back to Earth?"

Vander shook his head. "I don't know of a way. Shiraz might be able to help you. He has an affinity with the Sen technology."

She clearly had no idea what he meant. She just blinked and then shook her head. "What am I supposed to do?"

"For now, you should stay with us at the fortress. We'll do our best to help you in any way we can." Virgo made the offer without looking at Vander for confirmation.

Vander wasn't concerned. He and Virgo were clearly of an accord on this. He wondered if Virgo felt the same pull toward the strange creature as he did? She had appeared at the moment in the ceremony where their mate or mates' charms would have lit up. Did that mean she was their mate to share? That wasn't uncommon among the Drakari, but someone like this Earth creature certainly was.

"I don't know where I am, or who you are. I can't do that."

Vander let out an impatient sigh. "The reality is, you can either stay here on the surface alone, or you can come back to the fortress with us and have a comfortable room while we try to help you figure out what's going on here." He spoke firmly, and he didn't soften his tone. She didn't need to know that he wouldn't leave her there on the surface alone. She probably knew nothing of their flora and fauna, and she'd die if they abandoned her. If he had to, he would physically take her back to the fortress, but he wanted to avoid that unpleasantness.

She hesitated for another moment, with her eyes still big in her face. "I guess I have no choice." She winced. "I don't mean to sound ungrateful, but I'm scared."

Vander's slight irritation with her softened, and he put a hand on her shoulder. He was pleased when she didn't flinch away this time. "We'll do our best to get to the bottom of this. In the meantime, let us take you somewhere comfortable, and you can tell us more about Earth."

She nodded, still looking uncertain. He was amused that when they slipped off the land and into the water, she took a big breath and appeared to be holding it when they were under the waves. "Breathe," he reminded her.

After a moment, she let out a large exhale, and when she breathed in again, she was clearly just fine. She seemed just as stunned as she had earlier, and she shook her head. "How did I just grow gills? None of this makes any sense."

"I'm sure there's a reason you're here," said Virgo. He sounded optimistic, and Vander could guess his brother had already decided this woman was to be their mate. Vander could hardly fault him for the conclusion, since he was leaning in that direction as well.

"It doesn't do any good to give in to the fear when you have no answers. Come with us, and we'll take care of you. I'm Vander, and this is Virgo."

"Eva," she said in a shaky voice. "Though my cyborg name would be E-V-A."

"What is a cyborg?" asked Vander as they swam toward the fortress, he and his brother both keeping a hand on her arms to guide her.

"They're enhanced humans, modified with technology to live practically forever. My father is a cyborg, and my mother technically is. She has cybernetic parts anyway."

Vander couldn't help a hiss of disgust. "You must be of Sen descent."

She frowned. "I don't know what you're talking about."

"Sen used to own this planet. They are monstrous hybrids of organic flesh and shining metal. They had modified themselves to be able to live almost forever as well. They were a cruel and evil race."

She blinked. "Well that's not me or my family. We're not cruel."

Virgo glared at him, and Vander realized he should have been less intense in his reaction. He managed a small smile. "That's good to know then." He couldn't imagine a worse fate than being paired with a Sen for a mate, though the Sen hadn't lived on Senufo for seven hundred years.

She seemed mollified by his acceptance, and she started looking around with wide-eyed wonder as they reached the fortress, opting to walk down the rock bridge that led inside, through the virtually impenetrable walls. "How is any of this possible?" She giggled suddenly, though there was slight edge of hysteria to it. "How am able to talk underwater without every sound being blub, blub, blub?"

He wasn't certain what she meant, so he just shrugged. "We talk intelligibly underwater."

She nodded her agreement as they passed through the shield. She had a noticeable response by the way she tensed, and he knew she must have felt the hum of power that Drakari felt when they breached the barrier. He and Virgo led her through the lower floor of the fortress, which had been drained of water. She seemed to relax as soon as they were past the shield that kept out the water when it wasn't wanted, clearly more comfortable out of water.

They paused to greet Barta, who stood in the Chiefs' Chamber. They approached her, though Eva seemed uncertain. Vander knew Barta had to give permission for Eva to stay. Since she'd been there when Eva appeared, he couldn't imagine she would deny her sanctuary, but he was tense at the thought. He didn't know what he'd do if Barta told him Eva had to leave the fortress.

"You seem much calmer now," said Barta directly to Eva.

Eva shuddered a little, but she firmed her shoulders. "I suppose."

"How did you come to be here?" asked Barta.

"I don't know. One moment, I was tending the garden and talking to my best friend Nyandra, and then my pendant lit up. It had never done that before. It was so bright it almost hurt my eyes." Her fingers danced lightly over the pendant as she spoke. "Then I was just here, and with gills." She sounded bewildered again. "How can this happen?"

"I have no answers for you," said Barta. "My nephew, Shiraz, might be of assistance. He has a good grasp on the Sen technology."

She nodded, still looking overwhelmed.

"I've invited her to stay with us at the fortress. Is that acceptable, Chief?" With the death of Barta's twin, Botham, two months ago, she was no longer First Chief or Second Chief. She was simply Chief.

Barta nodded. "I would like to speak more with you, but rest now and settle in. We'll find a way to help you if we can."

Eva's eyes blinked rapidly. "Thank you."

With a nod from Barta, he and Virgo directed her away from the Chief's Chamber and up a set of stairs. Many of the Drakari in their tribe lived inside the fortress, because it was safe and fortified. Just because they hadn't been to war with the fellow tribes for the last hundred planetary cycles didn't mean the peace would last.

By unspoken agreement, he and Virgo took her to the fourth floor, finding a free room just across the hall from the Chief's quarters, which would soon be theirs. It made him nervous to think of her out of his sight, though the reaction was illogical.

Virgo opened the door for her, showing her how to use the panel in the rocks to do so. Then they led her in. It was a modest chamber, but she still seemed to find it interesting. She glanced around with wonder. "I don't know why, but I expected this room to have water." She gave a laugh that sounded self-conscious.

Vander walked closer to her. "The fortress is contained within the water, but protected by a shield the water doesn't pass through unless programmed to do so. Our ceremonies are done underwater, but we usually keep the fortress free of the ocean for daily living." He hoped she didn't ask why they held ceremonies in water, because he didn't know. It was just the way the tribes had always done things, at least after the Sen.

She seemed impressed. "Thank you. Would it be all right if I had some time to myself?"

Vander was reluctant to leave her, but he couldn't deny her reasonable request. He nodded as Virgo said, "We'll return for you later to take you to a meal, if you'd like?"

She shrugged. "I'm not sure what I want at this point, but of course you should come and ask me to see if I'm up for it." She smiled at both of them. "I can't thank you enough for your kindness."

Vander grunted, feeling a little guilty. She seemed to think they were being so kind just because they were compassionate about her situation. While he would've worried about anyone who'd suddenly appeared in their midst and seemed so frightened, he was certain he wouldn't have taken such a hands-on role for just anyone.

He could feel a connection to her, though it wasn't clear if she felt anything at all for him or Virgo yet. Perhaps that would develop in time, if she wasn't feeling it now. He certainly hoped so, because he was more and more convinced with each moment he'd spent with her that Eva was meant to be his and Virgo's mate.

Chapter 2

AS SOON AS THEY LEFT the chamber, Eva found what must be the bathroom, and she was able to figure it out with some careful experimentation. She stripped out of her sodden clothes and traded them for what looked like a cloth tube hanging on the back of the door. She put it over her head and discovered the fabric moderately shaped itself to her curves. It was like wearing a sleeveless sundress, though lighter.

Leaving the restroom, she collapsed on the bed. Her head was spinning, and she could hardly believe the events that had taken place. Where was she, and how had she come to be here? And who were those gorgeous green men with taut bodies and an imposing air of strength.? One had purplish black hair, and the other had more of a maroon-black hair, and they didn't look much alike in features, but something about the two of them suggested they were a matched set. She couldn't imagine one without the other.

She grasped the pendant again, convinced it had something to do with her arrival here. Which meant this was all linked to Freydon. "Freydon Rote, can you hear me? If this is your doing, please talk to me."

With a shimmer of silver, a peachy gelatinous blob appeared in front of her. He wore a black and white crocheted hat that had seen better days. That was the only familiar Earth thing about him. Otherwise, he seemed completely foreign, just like the Drakari who had rescued her. She glared at him. "What have you done?"

"I've done my job, dear. Your mates are here, and your pendant was calibrated to bring you to Senufo at the proper time."

She glared at him. "Mates? What are you talking about?"

"Vander and Virgo are your mates. I've seen it, and as you know if you've listened to your parents, I exist outside of time and space. I can see all possibilities infinitely, and I find matches for mates who would otherwise be apart."

"I've heard the stories," she said impatiently. "I know how you disrupted my mom and Penny's lives to bring them into the future and thrust them into the middle of a cybernetic war."

Freydon chuckled. "That's one way to look at it. Your mother is happy, isn't she?"

Eva gave him a grudging nod, having to concede that point. Normally, she found the story romantic, though she had doubted upon occasion the veracity of it. Now, she was confronted with her own peach blob, determined to meddle in her life, and she wasn't thrilled. "I want to go back to Earth. There are a number of handsome humans and cyborgs that I'll be happy to take as mates." There were even a couple of unmated male Grecopans, but they were elderly and infertile, thanks to the virus that had decimated the Grecopan population before Freydon brought them to Earth previously to her birth.

Freydon shook his head. "I'm afraid you wouldn't be as happy with them as you will be with Vander and Virgo. You need to accept your lot."

She glared at him. "What does that mean?"

"It means you're here, and this is your new home. You should adjust to it, dear Eva. I know it seems unfair at the moment, but you will be grateful at some point."

She let out a sound of frustration. "I won't be grateful for you transporting me to... Where are we?"

"Senufo, and you're among the Drakari people. Your mates are warlords, though their race is peaceful these days and will remain so with the other tribes. Vander and Virgo will be taking over the Chiefdom soon."

Eva rubbed her for head, overwhelmed by all the information he was throwing at her. "None of this makes sense, and I choose not to be here."

"I'm terribly sorry, my dear, but this is where you are, and this is where you will stay." Freydon nodded to her and then bowed in a sweeping gesture before disappearing with the same shimmer of light.

"You little..." She trailed off, realizing she was talking to an empty room. Rote was gone, and there was no telling if she'd see him again. If he was telling her the truth, she was stuck here now, expected to accept two mates that she didn't even know. Who had two mates? She couldn't even fathom that. Where she lived, people had one mate, and that was it. She couldn't think of anyone who'd ever had a triad relationship. It was just unheard of in their culture.

Despite her mental resistance to the idea, she couldn't deny she was slightly intrigued by the idea. She had little trouble imagining Vander and Virgo without the shiny black pants they wore. Their chests were already revealed, and though green, they were well-sculpted and certainly attractive.

She let out a groan of annoyance. Was she really thinking about such things when she was trapped on an alien planet? What a ridiculous waste of time. She had to find a way off the planet, and she hoped the Shiraz person mentioned to her would be her ticket away from Senufo and back to Earth.

SHE WOKE WHAT MUST'VE been hours later, unaware of having fallen asleep. There was a knock at the door, and once she recognized what it was, she called, "Just a minute." Her head felt fuzzy, but she was able to stand up and stagger to the door, remembering how to open it after Virgo's tutorial.

She wasn't surprised to see Vander and Virgo standing in front of her. She remembered they were going to come to see if she wanted to eat dinner. Her stomach was empty, but she was nervous about appearing in public with more of the Drakari. "I'm not sure I feel like going for dinner—"

"This is breakfast," said Vander. "You must eat."

Virgo's tone was softer. "When we came last night to see if you wanted dinner, there was no answer."

Her mouth dropped open for a second. "I must've fallen asleep. Would it be possible just to get a tray here?"

Vander wore a stubborn expression. "No. You must meet the others, or you'll continue to feel lost and alone. Besides, Shiraz is expecting to meet with you today."

With a sigh, she looked down at her tube. "Can I wear this?" Seeing Virgo's quickly smothered smile, she intuited doing so would be like wearing a bathrobe to a communal meal at the base's mess hall. "Never mind. Let me change."

She padded into the bathroom, finding the clothes she'd worn yesterday had mostly dried while hanging on the hook. She slipped off the tube garment to put on the white pants and shirt, which both appeared stained. She must have encountered something either on the surface of Senufo or in the garden on Earth. They would have to do.

She returned to them a moment later, and she swore they both eyed her with appreciation, even in her loosely fitting, stained work clothes.

"Are you ready?" asked Vander.

With a nod, she followed them from the room, and they led her down the corridor and then another. She was soon lost and turned around, so she was glad to have them escorting her as they led her back to the main floor of the fortress, and into a room that was clearly their dining area. There were more Drakari inside than she could count, and she stumbled in the doorway. Her hair fell over her face when she ducked her head, and she appreciated the screen that shielded her slightly from curious eyes.

"Why don't you find her a place to sit, Virgo, and I'll grab food?" said Vander.

Virgo nodded, taking her hand to lead her to a table that had other Drakari already. She would've rather sat alone with Virgo and Vander, and she recognized they had already become somewhat of a security blanket for her. She trembled as he showed her to a chair, and she sat down. He joined her a moment later, and there was another space on her side, presumably for Vander.

Two women who looked almost identical sat at the table. The main difference was one had cherry-red hair, and the other had a more sedate lavender shade. Their features were almost the same, though the one with cherry hair had a more delicate nose. She was certain they were sisters.

"This is Thana and Tarra, who are our childhood friends," said Virgo. "We were born at the same time."

"All of you at once?" She was confused.

"Within days of each other." That clarification came from the woman with lavender hair. Her skin was a moss-green shade, just like her twin's.

"So, you're both twins, and Virgo and Vander are twins?" asked Eva.

The woman with lavender hair nodded. "Thana was born a few minutes before me, but yes, we're twins. Drakari typically have twins or triplets. A singleton is a rare occurrence, but it's a cause for celebration. They've been marked for something special to be born alone. Fate is repaying them for the loss of the support of a twin by giving them a greater destiny."

Eva nodded, struggling not to show she thought that was nonsense. It sounded very mystical to her, and she didn't believe in magic or anything like fate. Still, she wasn't about to insult them or their culture.

She just nodded as Vander appeared, setting down a heaping tray on the table. She looked closer at the table, realizing it was some kind of shell. It was beautiful, but the food awaiting her wasn't.

Beautiful was the last word she would use to describe the odd bits of gelatinous-looking substances. She recognized it all as vaguely seafood-like, and she only knew that from her education. The Earth they were rebuilding didn't yet have enough balance restored to the oceans to clone the DNA of the sea creatures stored in the Ark and release the resulting beings.

Not wanting to be rude, she selected a bit with her fingers after watching Vander and Virgo do the same. She brought it to her face, sniffing cautiously. It had a strange, robust scent she didn't recognize, with the underlying tang of salt.

Taking a deep breath, she put it in her mouth and started to chew. The texture was off-putting, but the flavor wasn't bad. She discovered most of the offerings on the tray were like that. They had a strange texture or smell, but they didn't taste bad. At least she wasn't going to starve to death or be forced to eat repulsive things until she could get back to Earth.

As they ate, Tarra asked her multiple questions, and Eva did her best to answer. Thana didn't say a word. She was too busy glaring at Eva every time their eyes met. Eva wondered if she was just generally xenophobic, or if there was more to her apparent dislike. Whatever the reason, Thana had clearly decided to hate Eva. That made her nervous, especially when Vander said, "We have things we must do to prepare for the Ascension ceremony, which will take place soon."

"I see."

"Thana and Tarra are going to show you around to make sure you aren't left alone today." Virgo said that in a way that sounded reassuring. "Shiraz is supposed to find you sometime today as well."

Eva intuited he must think being alone was the worst thing ever. In a society where one was born in pairs or more, it was unsurprising they wouldn't like to be alone. She didn't want to sit in her room all day trying to think of a way home, but she wasn't certain she wanted to be paraded around the fortress either. Tarra seemed pleasant enough, but Thana was clearly not looking forward to the prospect of keeping her company.

Still, she couldn't think of a gracious way to decline, so she managed to force a smile. "How thoughtful of you to arrange that."

"We have to go. We'll see you later this afternoon," said Vander. He seemed reluctant to leave her, as did Virgo.

Eva realized she was just as reluctant for them to be gone. Now that her mind had cleared from sleep, she realized she had missed them. As they moved away, she already felt bereft again. What was going on?

"Now that they're gone, I have things to do," said Thana. They were practically the first words she'd spoken.

Eva shrugged as Tarra gasped. "You told Vander and Virgo you would help look after Eva today."

Thana glared briefly at her sister before turning a more scorching glower on Eva. "I don't know what that thing is, or how it came to be here, but I want no part of it." With a toss of her cherry-red hair, she stood up and strode away.

Tarra looked awkward for a moment, and Eva felt the same. What could she say? It wasn't like she could comment on Thana being a bitch, at least not to her twin sister.

After a moment, Tarra relaxed. "I apologize. Thana was convinced she would be a mate for either Virgo or Vander, or perhaps even both. It's what she set her heart on, though there was no indication it would happen. There's never an indication until the ceremony, though of course, there's often an attraction before confirmation."

"Was she in love with one or both?" The thought made her teeth clench with jealousy as she tried to piece together what Tarra was telling her. She must mean some Drakari were attracted to each other even before some voodoo ceremony confirmed they were the ones meant to be together.

Tarra's eyes widened, and she giggled. "Oh, not at all. They're like brothers to us."

"Then why...?"

"She wants to be Chief, but I have no interest, so I refused to join her in the trials. One alone can't compete unless born a singleton. She decided to settle for being the mate of a Chief when we were still young."

It was reassuring to know Thana was after power, not love, with Vander and Virgo, but she refused to analyze why. "I don't know why she's concerned. I'm not here to mate Vander or Virgo." She ignored the niggle of doubt in the back of her mind, put there by Freydon's assurance that she was where she belonged.

Tarra looked skeptical, but she didn't call her on it. Instead, she said, "Would you like to come with me to the shops? We can get you a few items of clothing. It didn't appear that you brought anything extra with you, after all."

Eva shook her head. "No, I didn't get a chance to bring anything." Her chest hurt for a moment as she imagined the fear and worry happening back at the base on Earth. Her parents would be frantic to know what had happened to her, as would her siblings and friends. Even the cyborgs, humans, and Grecopans she wasn't particularly close to would be worried about her.

Eva could freely acknowledge she was something of a spoiled princess among her family back on Earth, partially because she had been the first baby born to the settlement in hundreds of years. People doted on her, and they would be frightened and worried about her disappearance. So was she, but she had no way to get hold of them and assure them she was okay.

At least so far, she was okay. Thana clearly didn't like her, but she could deal with that. Right now, she had a roof over her head and food, though it might not be her first choice, and she had people who seemed to want to be her friend, or at least help her out.

As she followed Tarra from the dining room in the pursuit of getting a new wardrobe, she admitted to herself that Vander and Virgo clearly wanted more than friendship. Apparently, they bought into the ceremony that decided she was their mate. She didn't care if Freydon Rote had a spotless track record. This time, he was certainly wrong, and she intended to return to Earth rather than surrender and accept two men as her mates. Even if they were fabulously attractive, and they made her mouth water when she stared at them, she wasn't going to do this. Eva controlled her own fate.

Chapter 3

EVA HAD BEEN ENCHANTING even in the strange garb she'd arrived in, but in the dress favored by the women of their tribe, Virgo could barely catch his breath at the sight of her. She still stood out, because her skin and her hair were different, but she stood out in a stunning way. He counted himself fortunate that she was to be his mate.

Glancing at his brother, Virgo bared his teeth slightly, shocked by a wave of jealousy that swept over him. He'd never expected to feel jealous about sharing a mate with his brother should they be destined to have one between them. It was such a commonplace arrangement, so how could he react that way to the idea of sharing his mate with his brother? It made no sense to him, and he made a concentrated effort to push aside the emotion, hoping it was just a transient thing.

He and Vander both rushed to her side, each taking her arm to escort her the rest of the way into the dining chamber. Tarra walked with her, but there was no sign of Thana. He asked Tarra, "Where's your sister?"

"I'm not certain. I haven't seen her all day." Tarra's lips were pursed, and she seemed disapproving.

He frowned slightly, wanting to ask more, but Barta entered the room then, and everyone stood in silence until she'd taken her seat at the head of the table, as was the custom. The seat that had belonged to Botham remained empty, as it had since his death, and Virgo stared at it for a moment, still finding it almost impossible to believe that chair would be his within the next month. Vander would sit on his right, in the spot designated for the elder twin. Had triplets been successful in winning the trials, a third seat would've been added at the head of the table for the third-oldest.

He realized he was explaining this to Eva as he seated her, helping her push in her chair. Vander looked irritated that he had beaten him to assisting her, but he sat without protest on her other side. Virgo took a seat beside her, having a difficult time keeping his hands to himself.

He wanted to touch her skin to see if it was as creamy and soft as it looked, as revealed by the *swara* preferred by the women of the tribe. He wanted to bury his hand in her hair to see if it was as soft and silky as it seemed. The gleaming black of it enticed his senses, but he resisted the urge to touch without her consent. Instead, he folded his hands into fists and rested them lightly on the table.

"How was your day with Tarra and Thana?" asked Vander.

Eva smiled, though her eyes looked a little strained. "I didn't see much of Thana. She was...busy. Tarra was a pleasant companion, and she showed me quite a few interesting things around the fortress."

"How are you settling in?" asked Virgo.

She looked at him, and the sadness in her eyes was enough to make his chest squeeze in sympathy. "It's very hard to say, since I just got here. Apparently, there's no way home, but I haven't accepted that."

"Did Shiraz tell you that?" asked Vander.

She shook her head. "I haven't seen him yet."

"You'll have to speak to Shiraz. There might still be hope," said Virgo, though the last thing he wanted to do was facilitate her ability to leave him. He barely knew her, but he knew on a deep, intuitive level that she was his mate.

Eva nodded at his words. "I hope to. I've heard from a few people now that he's the one who might help me be able to figure out how to get home."

Virgo didn't like the idea of her going anywhere, and he clutched his hands in tighter fists to hold back his visible anger at the idea. The beast that lived inside the heart of every Drakari warrior rebelled at the idea of his mate leaving. It urged him to take her from the dining chamber to the nearest room where they could be alone, so he could claim her.

The beast inside snarled at the idea of Vander joining them, and the unwelcome surge of jealousy was what helped him quell the urge to do as instinct demanded. He breathed deeply and waited for it to pass. When it finally had, and he was calm enough to speak again, he said, "You should come to our chambers after the meal."

Her eyes widened, and she looked offended. "I don't think so."

"He didn't mean that," said Vander. "Barta gave us the Chiefs' suite today, and we just moved in."

Virgo held up a hand. "We have the best view of the Byzanian Abyss. You don't want to miss it."

She eyed him for a moment before relaxing slightly, apparently deciding he was being truthful. He didn't like that she would question his honor, but she didn't yet know him. It was up to him to prove to her he was a worthy mate.

"It's a breathtaking view," said Vander. Then he engaged her in conversation about her life on Earth, and Virgo tried to get in the conversation as much as possible. He wanted her undivided attention and having to share with Vander made him feel like a sulking child.

When the meal ended, Eva walked between them to the stairs, and they ascended the four floors with her between them. Virgo wanted to do more than hold her arm lightly, but he reined in the impulse. He was a warrior with savage instincts, but he was also civilized enough to control his baser impulses.

When they reached the chambers he now shared with Vander, he pushed open the door, and they entered. It still delighted him with its newness and luxury, and it clearly had the same effect on Eva. She paused in mid-step and a gasp escaped her. "It's magnificent."

"It is," said Vander.

Virgo could view it through her eyes, since it was new to him too. He was used to their architecture that incorporated organic materials, including the stone that jutted from the floor of the ocean, along with a Sen metal alloy that provided support and structure. It gleamed through, causing a shimmer in some parts of the rock around them.

They were on the upper floor of the chamber when they entered, and the spiral set of stairs led to the lower quarters, which contained their living area and sleeping spaces. This floor had the balcony, and Virgo tugged lightly on her arm to get her to walk with him.

Vander was left with the choice of either letting go or coming along, and of course, he clung to her. It's what Virgo would've done as well, but he was still resentful that his brother was there. He disliked being at odds with him, and he wondered if Vander was feeling the same thing, or if he remained blissfully unaware of the jealousy seething below the surface.

"Here's the view we promised," said Vander as he opened the doors to the balcony. All-econmpassing water faced them, but it didn't seep into the room, due to the preset controls. They swept outside, and the currents were strong this evening. Her hair immediately flitted around her face, and tendrils teased his face. He brushed them away gently as they took her to the edge of the balcony.

She gasped again, this time perhaps with some fear. They were hundreds of meters from the floor of the ocean, and thousands of meters from the depth of the Byzanian Abyss. They couldn't possibly see the bottom from here. It went so deep that even the Drakari, genetically modified as they were, couldn't withstand the pressure of the trench.

What made it magnificent was all the bioluminescent life that survived in the abyss. They sparkled and shone, and it was like looking at the sky when they were above the surface. Even looking up, he could see the sky through the fathoms of water separating him from the surface, but it was hazy and blurred. When he looked down into the abyss, the images were crisp and clear.

She let out a startled cry and stepped back, clutching her chest.

Virgo frowned. "Are you ill?"

She shook her head as she lifted a hand, and he noticed it was trembling. It took him a moment to realize she was pointing at a *bvago*. He relaxed his guard and smiled at her. "That's a *bvago*."

"What's that?" She seemed captivated by the glowing purple and green sea creature. It was just a juvenile, so was only around fifty meters longer.

"It's a harmless creature. You had some of it for dinner this evening."

She looked paler than she had a moment before, and she gulped. "It looks a lot scarier than you're making it sound."

"The spikes are dull-edged," said Vander. "They're actually made of cartilage, and the innards are used in some of our desserts."

"The tongue is the true delicacy," said Virgo. "That was the grayish purple meat on your plate this evening."

She looked a little ill as she took a couple of deep breaths. "It was really tasty, but seeing that up close like this..." She shuddered. "We eat mostly a vegetarian diet."

"What does that mean?" asked Vander.

"We don't usually slaughter animals for food. We're still terraforming and trying to rebuild the populations of all the animals, so it's rare that we sacrifice some of our stock to eat it."

Virgo shrugged. "The *bvago* are common, and we have no fear of them reaching extinction. That's just a juvenile, and we don't harvest until they're adults. One can be up to three hundred meters and feeds all of the tribe for a few meals."

Eva nodded, and then she froze. "I just realized you speak my language, or I speak yours. How's that possible?"

"I don't know," said Vander, casting a glance at Virgo.

He shrugged, having no clue either. "Perhaps it has something to do with the modifications the Sen did to us."

"What modifications? I've heard several mentions of Sen, but I still don't know exactly who they are, besides they were the original dwellers of the planet," said Eva.

"They kidnapped us from our home world, which is across the galaxy, and they modified each Drakari survivor to be able to breathe and live underwater to function as their slaves." Virgo virtually spat out the last word, feeling the instinctive race-deep surge of hatred that every Drakari bore the Sen.

"What happened to them?"

"Our people rebelled several generations ago, and we wiped them out." Vander didn't bother to hide his pride in their accomplishment. "They had technology, and an amazing amount of it, but we had numbers and something they never anticipated."

"What's that?" asked Eva.

"The thirst for freedom, and the need to control our own destinies. Drakari are a strong and independent people, and we didn't adapt well to slavery."

"Is that why you live in this modern structure with capabilities I'm not even able to guess about, and yet have a different, more basic societal structure?"

Virgo laughed. "I believe she's implying we're primitive, brother."

Vander laughed as well as Eva turned bright red. "That wasn't what I meant."

Virgo patted her lightly on the shoulder. "Don't worry. We aren't offended in the least. It's true that Drakari were several stages behind in our civilization compared to the Sen, but since there's no way to return to our original planet, we've adapted to this one. We fit their technology into our culture as best as we could and have emerged stronger for it. Some of us are better than others with the Sen technology."

Eva nodded. "Like Shiraz? I hear he's got a special affinity with the Sen technology?"

"That's correct," said Vander. "We'll make sure you meet with him soon, so he can see what your possibilities are, if you're determined to return to this place called Earth."

Her expression softened. "It's still a rough place to live. My people did a horrible job of managing the planet, and even actively destroyed it in an attempt to destroy the cyborgs they were fighting against. If it hadn't been for Freydon Rote bringing the Grecopan terraformers to our planet, Earth would still be a desolate place.

"There are large swaths of the planet that are still uninhabitable, but we're rebuilding from our settlement outward. They reached Alaska last year and found another enclave there, and the technology has spread. Someday, Earth will be as beautiful and lush as it once was. It might not be much to look at now, but it's my home." A note of melancholy bled through her tone. "My family will be very worried, and I have no way to even contact them."

"Perhaps Shiraz will know a way," said Vander.

Virgo frowned at him. He figured his brother was just trying to soothe Eva and remove her sadness, but he didn't like her having false hope. Shiraz understood many of the Sen gadgets, but he doubted Barta's nephew had a grasp on how to send interplanetary messages. As far as Virgo knew, there was no way that existed. If so, it was one of the secrets that remained undiscovered about the Sen technology.

When she had tired of looking at the abyss, Virgo took her arm to lead her inside. He stiffened when she stumbled to a halt and gasped. "What's wrong?"

"My dress-thing...*swara*? It's dry. No wonder Tarra said I'd love it." She seemed stunned, but pleased, judging from the small smile on her face.

He settled her on the sofa near the balcony, not suggesting they go down to the living quarters. He sat with her as he asked, "Would you like something to drink?"

"Do you have tea?"

Virgo nodded, and Vander appeared with a tray a minute later. That must've been where his brother had disappeared to when they came in from the balcony. Had he read their mate's preferences so well so soon when Virgo had yet to get a sense of her? When they joined, he would be able to read her easier. It wasn't that he was psychic, but Drakari were good at picking up pheromones and subtle variations of the person's body that revealed how they were feeling. The strongest mate bonds even allowed some sense of how their mate was feeling across distances.

Mostly, he got uncertainty and the occasional wave of fear from Eva so far. Since he wanted to see nothing but smiles on her face, it troubled him to know she was so sad and confused.

Vander poured her a cup of the moth-lace tea. She took a sip before making a sound of appreciation and taking another. "What is it?"

"It's moth-lace tea." Virgo reached for a cup for himself. "The moth-lace live in complicated webs on the surface. Their tea is prized, and not just because it's difficult to obtain. Moth-lace are so delicate that the slightest brush of our fingers against them will kill them. If we kill them, they'll no longer produce the web that makes the tea, and then we'll all be without the delicacy, and we'll have the death of all the moth-lace on our hands."

"Tarra's a skilled harvester of moth-lace." Vander took a long sip. "I know you must have a deft hand and a gentle outlook to be able to harvest parts of the web without taking so much that the moth-lace die, and while also avoiding touching them. Perhaps she could show you the skill, if you're interested?"

Eva looked down at her cup of tea, and she appeared unsettled. "This is insect web?"

Virgo nodded. "Perhaps I can show you where they nest tomorrow. We could go for a walk?"

Vander scowled at him. "Not without me."

"It's only proper to have time alone with our mate to woo her." Virgo glared at his brother.

"Since when do we woo separately? We're a team."

She held up a hand as their argument started to escalate. "Please don't be offended, but I'm not here to be wooed. I just want to get home." She sounded sincere, but she looked a little uncertain.

"We would already be bonded in the traditional mating ceremony if you were of our kind." Vander seemed to think that settled the issue, and Eva should just accept that.

Virgo was more sensitive. He patted her lightly on the arm. "Vander's not trying to rush you. He's just letting you know that by now, we would've all consummated our union if this were normal circumstances."

"I'm not consummating anything with anyone. I want to get home, not be stuck here." She winced at the way they both flinched. "I'm sorry. I didn't mean it that way, of course. Senufo seems like a lovely planet, but it's not my home. I'm not sure why I'm here—"

"You're here to be our mate," said Vander with crushing logic that dared her to argue.

She just shook her head. "Until I find a way home, I appreciate your hospitality, but I can't be anyone's mate."

"Surely you can spend time with us and try to get to know us?" asked Virgo.

After a moment, Eva nodded. "I'd enjoy that, but I don't want you to expect something that's never going to happen."

"A mating is never forced. In the rare occasions when matches haven't been compatible, or one partner has no interest in the other, either the bonding is severed with a simple ceremony, or it never takes place to start with." Virgo explained the dynamics to her as quickly and briefly as he could.

She hesitated and then nodded. "I'd like to go on that walk with you tomorrow, Virgo."

He couldn't keep from smiling widely. "I'd like that as well. I have duties to attend to, in preparation for the Ascension, but I'll make sure to have some free time for you in the afternoon, and I'll find you then."

A hint of color came to her cheeks, and she seemed to flush with pleasure at the idea. She gave him a smile that appeared somewhat shy as she nodded her head. "I look forward to it."

Vander looked unhappy, but he didn't argue. He just sat stoically on the loveseat closest to Eva. A spark of conscience twanged through Virgo, and he nearly offered for Vander to come along. Only the realization that he wanted all the time he could have with Eva to himself held him back.

Chapter 4

AFTER A SEMI-SLEEPLESS night, where Eva constantly turned over in her mind her options, and concluded she had very few, she woke with a headache and a sour outlook. She wasn't in the best mood when Virgo came to her room to meet her for their walk.

She tried to hide her unpleasant mood as they started walking, with him pointing out the various sites in the fortress. She'd already seen a few of them with Tarra, but she it was all so different from Earth as to remain intriguing.

She heard the shouts and laughter of children ahead and looked at Virgo. "What's that?"

"It's just the park. Would you like to see it?"

She nodded, having nothing else to do at the moment. If she was going to be stuck here, she'd have to find some kind of useful purpose. She was an expert on Earth plants and soil, but she doubted that would translate well to the vegetation she'd seen growing in the fortress and in the ocean beyond.

They turned right at the next corridor, and it wasn't far until they reached the park. It was an open space with play equipment that looked surprisingly similar to the swings and slides set up for the children at their base back home. Part of it was submersed in water, but they chose the side without water.

"How do you keep the water in half the room? I don't see a wall separating the sides." Eva craned her head, but she couldn't see a visible barrier.

"There's a shield in here, like there is outside the fortress. This was where the Sen first kept the Drakari when they brought them to this world. They were trapped in here, but without water, since my kind couldn't originally breathe underwater. Once they were modified, they were kept on the other side of the enclosure, where the water is. We keep it this way to remember our origins and honor our ancestors."

They sat on a bench nearby to watch the children play for a bit, and she found it lightened her mood. They were all so joyful and just happy with the simplest things, like being pushed on the swing. It certainly didn't alleviate the worries of her situation, and it couldn't take away her desire to return home, but it was difficult to remain in such a dour mood when others around her were filled with happiness.

"Do you want children?" asked Virgo.

She shrugged a shoulder. "I suppose. It's certainly something I've considered, but there wasn't really anyone back home who caught my attention. I figured I would meet someone at the right point, though I know everybody in our little colony. I was hopeful that maybe someone in the Alaskan base would be a match." She shrugged, not able to convey how little thought she'd given it. Some of her contemporaries had already paired up and had children, but most of them were focused on rebuilding Earth, just like she was, and romance had taken a distant second.

"Vander and I both want children with our mate." His words were meaningful, and he slid a bit closer. When he reached for her hand, she didn't jerk away.

She thought about doing so, but not because she didn't want to hold his hands. It was because she was attracted to him, and she didn't want to risk further complicating her situation by falling for her supposed mates. That might keep her from wanting to return home, and she couldn't allow that.

Still, holding his hand was nice, and they moved closer together by mutual agreement. He put his arm around her shoulders, and she leaned lightly against him. "This planet is amazing, but I don't think I'd ever get used to being underwater."

"You wouldn't be most of the time." Virgo shrugged. "For me, it's the opposite. I love the ocean, though I spend most of my time in the fortress, like every other Drakari. When I'm on the surface, I feel out of my element."

"A fish out of water?" she teased.

His eyes widened, and he apparently knew what fish was for an Earthling. He laughed after a moment and nodded. "That's not the most flattering comparison, but I suppose it's accurate."

"I just don't understand how Freydon Rote thought this would work." She shook her head.

Virgo stiffened. "What is Freydon Rote?"

She realized she hadn't yet shared the information she'd acquired with him or Vander. "He's a Celestial Mates agent. Supposedly, he exists outside of time and space and can make matches across galaxies and timelines for mates who never would've met otherwise. In my opinion, he's a meddlesome little blob."

Virgo shook his head. "I don't understand."

She tried to explain a little better and then added, "He's the one who matched my parents. He brought my mother four hundred years into the future on our planet, and it was a war zone. Earth was dying, and the humans and cyborgs were at war with each other and both at war with these things called synthetics. It was before my time, but I guess the synths didn't have any compassion or ability to reason. They were just pure machines. Believe it or not, my mother and father getting together ended the war with the humans, and they became allied. Then they defeated the synths, and Freydon brought a group of aliens who specialize in terraforming to our world . The Grecopan are also green, but a paler shade, and they have pointed ears. We've all lived in harmony ever since. Blah, blah, blah."

"You don't sound sincere."

She let out a sigh. "Oh, I am, actually. We have a good thing now, and that really is thanks to Freydon, but I never expected him to thrust me into this kind of situation. He should've just ended his meddling with my parents and let it go at that."

She understood her parents both had great affection for Freydon, but she had a feeling that might change if they ever learned his role in her disappearance. Having grown up listening to stories of him, all tinged with affection, it did make her feel a little guilty to be talking badly about the small peach alien, but she was angry at him for trying to dictate her destiny.

"So, you're saying he brought you here?" Virgo's tone revealed little.

She nodded. "He came to me the first night of my arrival and explained he brought me here to find my mates. There's no way home, so he told me to just live with it. That's not me though. I need to find a way back to Earth and my family."

Virgo frowned. "We could be your family here. If you're supposed to be our mate, you know Vander and I would take care of you and cherish you."

That sounded tempting, but she hardened her heart. "Thank you for the offer, but this isn't where I belong." She could see the hurt on his face, so she looked away quickly. Her gaze settled on a father pushing his child in the swing, her mind insisting on imagining what a child with Vander and Virgo would look like.

Recalling they mostly had twins or triplets, she'd have to multiply that by two or three. That was a daunting prospect, and it made it a little easier to banish the image. She cleared her throat and started to stand. "We should probably get back." Not that she had anything planned, but she needed some distance before she succumbed to the temptation Virgo represented.

"If you don't mind, there's one more place I'd like to show you first." At her nod, he held out his hand.

Eva took it reluctantly, feeling the *zap* when their hands touched again. There was no denying her attraction to both Virgo and Vander, but it still didn't seem like enough to give up contact with her family and live in this strange place.

They returned to the corridor and headed the opposite direction, taking a couple more turns before he led her into a room filled with books. She recognized the format easily enough, though the materials were obviously different. She reached for the closest one and flipped it open. The pages were light-green, and the font was a darker green. Before her eyes, they turned from gibberish to words she could read. "How is that possible?"

Virgo arched a purplish eyebrow. "How is what possible?"

"That I can read the text? It went from being symbols that meant nothing to English."

He frowned. "It's written in Sen. It took us a long time to figure out their language. They used a more formal language for books and among each other than they used to address the slaves. Perhaps it's something that Freydon Rote did to you when he gave you gills and altered your skin?"

She nodded. "Perhaps." Then she froze. "What do you mean, altered my skin?"

He frowned. "Haven't you noticed your skin is starting to turn light-green? It's probably the thin protective film that develops on Drakari to keep our skin protected from the salinity of the water."

She lifted a hand, shocked to see there was definitely a green tinge to her skin. It reminded her of the shade of the Grecopan, who were lighter than the Drakari, but still darker than her—so far. Her pigment was still light and faintly noticeable, but she couldn't believe she hadn't observed it earlier. Her thoughts had been elsewhere, and she hadn't spent much time on her appearance.

"Does that mean I'm going to turn green?" She couldn't help sounding horrified. The people around her were beautiful and exotic with their green skin, but that didn't mean she wanted to be green too.

Virgo shrugged. "I have no answer for you. I do know Drakari weren't originally green before we were brought here." He walked across half the length of the library to select a book before returning. He opened it up for her, saying, "This is a log of the different species the Sen had enslaved over the years. Most weren't hardy enough to survive long-term, but the Drakari thrived even under the circumstances. We remained fertile and strong after they modified our DNA. From what the book says, most of the species no longer retained fertility after being modified, so they were a one-generation workforce."

Eva shuddered at the thought of a race who could enslave others, knowing it was a death sentence after one generation, but doing so just the same. The Sen must have been an awful "civilization."

She took the book from him, flipping through slowly. There were pictures for each race, and she saw a wide array of aliens she'd never imagined existed. Some of the races had photographs documenting their change, and she saw most of them ended up taking on a green or greenish tinge. It must have something to do with the protective coating Virgo had mentioned.

She gasped when she opened and flipped to the next page and saw an original Drakari. They had gleaming brown skin and dark hair. There was also a picture of that subject following genetic modification, and she could see the green protective film starting to flourish and take over the original dark-brown skin tone. The hair had changed as well, taking on a violet undertone.

Without thought, she lifted a hand to her black hair. "Is my hair changing too?"

He shrugged and moved closer, looking at it for a long moment. "I think it's taking on a blue undertone. It's still beautiful."

She nodded, but it was difficult to remain calm. How was she supposed to accept these changes in herself?

Abruptly, she recalled her mother telling her she hadn't always had cybernetic parts. It was after she was attacked by a synth that their doctor, OWN, had saved Carrie's life by integrating cybernetic parts with her human form, leaving her with sections of blue skin and the luminescent veins underneath that powered her circuitry. Her mother had adapted, and Eva had never seen her without patches of blue skin. If her mother could do it, she could too, but she was still angry and upset that everything about her would change.

She blinked back tears. "I didn't expect any of this. It's so unfair." Her emotions got the better of her, and she suddenly burst into tears. She started to turn away from Virgo, but he turned her toward him instead. She surrendered to the comfort he offered, leaning against him as his arms came around her. He stroked her hair, and he whispered sounds that soothed her, though she didn't recognize any words.

When she regained control, she lifted her head from his chest and looked up at him, mouth opened. She was about to thank him for his kindness, but his lips descended before she had a chance.

When they touched hers, it was like fireworks exploding between them. He consumed her, and she instinctively moved closer to him, tangling her hands into his hair. It was longer than hers, and she couldn't resist the urge to hold onto it and tug him closer.

His hands were on her buttocks, cupping her and lifting her against him, and she clung to Virgo as his tongue slipped into her mouth. She welcomed it with relish, stroking with her own as they feasted on each other. It wasn't her first kiss, but it was the first kiss that had ever made her feel like this. Her entire body was alive, with every nerve ending singing, and her compulsion to mate with him was almost irresistible.

Realizing how close she was to asking him to join with her caused her to turn her head and take a deep breath. It helped restore some perspective, and she managed to ease away from him slightly. She gave him a shaky smile, but she couldn't bring herself to speak. She was afraid if she did, she'd beg him to take her right then.

An image of Vander popped into her head, and she couldn't help wondering how his kisses would be. She could see herself between the two of them as they both lavished her with pleasure, and she shivered in delight at the idea. She didn't want to stay on Senufo, but the two of them certainly gave her persuasive reasons for why she might.

Virgo gave her a wry grin, seeming to realize the moment had passed. "Unfortunately, I have to return to my duties. Would you like me to return you to your room?"

She shook her head, not wanting to be cooped up with her own thoughts in the room. Instead, she opted to return to the main room of the fortress, and she was pleased to see Tarra sitting at a table. She walked over to join her, fascinated to see Tarra was doing something with what looked like fish bones and beads. Before she had a chance to ask what Tarra was doing, someone approached.

She stiffened at the thin man before her. He was green, but his color was more of a sickly yellow-green rather than the vibrant green both Vander and Virgo had, though of differing shades. Unlike most of the men she'd seen, he didn't have long hair. His was short and cropped tightly against his skull. It had an orange-red undertone, as did the pointed beard sprouting from his chin. She managed to smile, trying to appear friendly enough, though his appearance had taken her by surprise. She felt awful for judging him by it, assuming he must have some kind of illness. "Hello."

He nodded his head in her direction. "I'm Shiraz. I would have met with you sooner, but I've been busy doing some research on your problem."

Her smile widened. "I've heard you're really good with Sen technology. Do you know a way I can get back to Earth?"

He looked like he was pondering it for a moment. "Come with me. I might know a way."

She walked behind him, getting a strange vibe. He seemed unwelcoming, though she could hardly fault him for that. If someone from another planet had been dropped into their midst, she might've felt unwelcoming as well. At the very least, she would've been wary and concerned for the safety of their enclave, and the people in it.

He led her up a series of stairs, and she was breathless by the time they reached the top. She looked out from a window, and she realized they must be in a turret of the fortress. "What's up here?"

"A Sen galactic node."

She followed him into a room surrounded by technology she didn't recognize. It was that same strange blend of organic and metal, but it dominated the space. "What's a galactic node?"

"From what we can figure, it's how they traveled to various planets. They opened wormholes with the nodes so they could invade a planet and steal its resources and people for slaves."

She shuddered. "They sound like a charming group. I'm glad the Drakari managed to conquer them."

"So am I, though they were a fascinating species. They were ruthless and determined to do whatever was necessary to ensure the survival of their species. As their fertility rates dropped, they started looking at outsiders to support their society."

"How do you know their fertility rates dropped?" she asked as she moved closer to one of the machines.

"I read all the books in the library. The Sen had a rich and varied culture, but for reasons they couldn't explain, they stopped being able to produce viable offspring, except in small numbers. The theory was their mechanical and genetic enhancements to prolong life had altered their DNA too much, but they weren't willing to sacrifice virtual immortality for the ability to have children. Their best and brightest minds tackled the subject but didn't find a solution, so their generals came up with another idea to keep the society functioning while they produced as many children as they could."

She looked at him, seeing admiration in his expression. "You seem to like these Sen people."

He shrugged. "I admire their will to survive, and their ingenuity. I don't agree with their methods, but yes, I do respect vast parts of their culture."

It seemed strange to her that he could do so when the Sen had enslaved his own people and taken them from their home planet, but she didn't want to argue with him, especially since he represented her best chance of getting home. "Have you figured out how these nodes work?"

He nodded. "I know how to use them to get to the pre-programmed coordinates, including the original Drakari home world."

"How did that go?" She could imagine the shocked people on the original home world.

He grimaced. "Not well. It had been hundreds of years since our abductions, and we looked very little like the original Drakari. We sent a delegation a few generations ago, but we were rebuffed. The original Drakari wanted nothing to do with us, and so we have claimed Senufo as our home world."

"That must have been difficult for your people." She could imagine how much hope the generations-ago Drakari might have pinned on reconnecting with their origins.

"Perhaps." Shiraz shrugged. "So we know how to use the node to get to destinations the Sen already traveled. We just don't know how to go anywhere outside the preset coordinates."

"Have you, or others, traveled to other destinations that are in the settings?"

Shiraz shook his head. "After that experience, the Chiefs decided no good could come from it. It's not forbidden, exactly, but no one has ever been able to get permission to travel. I'm sure they would make an exception for you to return where you *belong*." There was definitely a note of anger under his words.

She suddenly realized she was alone with him up here. It shouldn't matter, but something about Shiraz was unsettling. Perhaps it was simply because he clearly didn't like her and didn't want her there. She eased a few steps back toward the door. "Have you found Earth in the presets?"

He looked disappointed. "I have not. I've only just started to understand how to open new worm holes at new coordinates using the node. I wanted to show you what we have and to assure you that I'm going to be working as hard as I can to find your planet for you."

She managed to smile. "I appreciate that."

"What can you tell me of your planet and solar system? Do you know your galaxy?"

She shrugged, struggling to remember those details from her education. The cyborgs had access to all of Earth's data that had survived, but since she wasn't a cyborg with a chip in her brain, she hadn't been able to instantly absorb that information. She'd had to learn it the old-fashioned way, via a teacher in the classroom. Those details hadn't seemed all that important to her when she was focused, even as a child, on restoring Earth to the glory of the pictures she'd seen in the classroom. Eventually, she remembered enough details that seemed to satisfy Shiraz.

"Thank you. With that information, I might be able to find your location easier, as long as it's in the Sen star charts. Their civilization lasted for millions of years, so it's quite likely that they got around to charting a good portion of the universes. I'll let you know when I know more."

She nodded her thanks and left the room. She ran down the first few flights of stairs, unable to explain why she wanted to be away from Shiraz but listening to instinct. As she slowed to a walk, she realized she hadn't mentioned the pendant to him. Despite what Freydon implied, she was still certain it was important and perhaps her only way home. She should've shown it to Shiraz and asked him to experiment to see if he could get it to do anything, like open a wormhole. Maybe the charm was a node itself.

The idea of turning around and going back to the room to offer it to Shiraz to look at made her uneasy. Her stomach clenched with nausea, and she kept going downward. If she were correct, she wanted to protect the pendant at all cost, and she didn't want to let it out of her sight. Shiraz might be able to help her find a way home using it, but her instincts screamed at her to protect it, so she kept walking away from him.

Chapter 5

THERE WAS A KNOCK ON her door later that afternoon, and she opened it to find Vander. He held out something that was recognizably the bloom of a flower, though she hadn't seen anything like it. She took it and brought it to her nose, inhaling its intoxicating scent. She couldn't think of anything it reminded her of on Earth, but she definitely loved the aroma. "What is it?"

"It's an *yzukan* water bloom. It's a traditional flower of courtship among Drakari who have not yet been matched with a mate."

"You mean affairs?" She asked, trying to understand.

He nodded. "Some Drakari wait years for their mating ceremony, and it gets lonely. There are alliances that are forged for mutual benefit in the interim."

She nodded her understanding. "Are you trying to set up a friends-with-benefits arrangement with me?"

He scowled. "Of course not. You're my mate. It was the meaning behind the flower that I'm trying to convey. I'm interested in you."

She smiled. "I admit I'm interested in you too." She almost mentioned Virgo, but this moment seemed to be about her and Vander. "What do you want from me, Vander?"

"I thought you might join me for dinner. Just the two of us?"

How could she deny his hopeful expression, especially when she had little desire to do so? "I'd be honored."

"I'll return for you in a few hours then. Thank you." He half-bowed toward her before standing up and moving away without looking back.

She closed the door to her room and wondered if she was making a mistake. She had agreed to keep them both company while she was stuck here, but if the evening with Vander left her as tempted as the morning with Virgo, it would just add to her confusion. Knowing it was probably not the best idea, she still couldn't bring herself to cancel on him.

HE ARRIVED A FEW HOURS later, as promised. She put on one of the *swara* in her closet that Tarra had helped her select. It was a rich red color, yet it didn't clash with the faint greenness of her skin. Her skin color appeared to be the same as earlier, so she had no idea how long it would be before she was entirely green, and a darker shade at that. When she returned to Earth, would the modifications Freydon made disappear on their own? If not, she was confident OWN would find a way to return her to the way she was.

Vander offered her his arm, and she slipped hers through his. They walked away from her room and down the corridor to a smaller room. This appeared to be something like a sitting room, though there was a table and two chairs arranged, along with food already waiting under cloches. She sat down with his assistance, and he moved across the table so he was looking right at her. The hunger in his gaze should've been unnerving, but all it did was ratchet up her own. Her mouth was dry, and she swallowed thickly. She was nervous and excited.

Vander lift the cloches off both their plates, and the menu appeared to be similar to last night's. She started eating as they talked for a bit about nothing consequential, and yet it somehow felt like every word was meaningful.

"I heard you met Shiraz today?" asked Vander. He sounded guarded.

She nodded. "Do you know about the nodes?" At his nod, she said, "He's going to see if he can find the coordinates for Earth, so we can open a wormhole there using the node. He could find it tomorrow, but as big as the universes are, I get the feeling it could take years." She blinked away moisture in her eyes.

"It could take a lifetime. You should focus on finding a way to be happy here." Vander sounded brusque.

She lifted a shoulder. "That might be my ultimate fate, but I can't give up just yet. I can't settle for this when I could go back to Earth."

Vander stiffened. "It's hardly settling to be the mate of the two Chiefs who are going to lead our tribe."

Seeing she'd offended him, she reached across the table and touched his hand. "I wasn't referring to you or Virgo. Being your mate wouldn't be settling for anything, I agree. It's just, this isn't where my I belong. I don't feel at home here, and my family and friends are on Earth. Surely you understand what I mean?"

His expression was grim, and his posture was stiff for a moment before he finally sighed and nodded. "I do understand, but the idea of you wasting years pursuing a way home that might not be possible when we could be bonded sends a pain through my chest." He clutched the left side for a moment. "My hearts clench at the idea."

"How many hearts do you have?" she asked, trying to distract him from the more serious topic.

"Three. One serves no function since the Sen modified us, though it was essential for life on our home world due to the low-oxygen atmosphere."

"Do they pump individually?" She was fascinated by the thought.

He shrugged. "I guess." He obviously didn't understand what she was asking.

"May I listen to your hearts?" At his nod, she rose from the table and moved to his side. He pushed back his chair, and she knelt on the floor between his splayed legs so she could press her ear to the left side of his chest. She could hear two distinct heartbeats, echoed by a third that sounded sluggish and low. "Does your third heart pump?"

"Yes, but it doesn't do anything."

She listened for another moment before starting to stand. As she got to her feet, Vander tugged on her hand until she was on his lap. She gasped at the contact and started to admonish him for overstepping his bounds, but she realized she didn't want to. Seated on him, snuggling close, the moment felt perfect. Before she could talk herself out of it, she lifted her head slightly so she could brush her lips against his.

Vander returned the kiss with enthusiasm, his tongue surging immediately into her mouth. He was a more aggressive and bolder kisser than Virgo, and it felt just right with him. So had the kiss with Virgo. Perhaps their styles complemented each other since they were destined to share a mate.

Vander cupped one of her breasts and squeezed lightly, brushing his fingers across her nipple as she clutched his shoulders and continued kissing him. It set fire to every cell in her body, and she writhed restlessly on his lap. She wanted to push aside the *swara* and take him inside her.

Realizing how quickly this was getting out of hand, she forced herself to break the kiss and scramble off his lap. She breathed heavily as she looked at him for a moment before clearing her throat and looking away. "We should probably get back to the others." That was a bald admission of how close she was to giving in.

"The communal meal will be done by now, but perhaps you'd like to join me in my suite for another view of the abyss? Virgo will be there too."

He was hardly a chaperone that would ensure she behaved herself, but she nodded. She'd spent time with both of them alone, but she couldn't deny that whatever she was feeling was magnified by a thousand when she was with the two of them together. Going with him to his suite was probably a stupid decision if she wanted to avoid becoming further involved with them, but she couldn't resist temptation.

They entered his suite via the balcony entrance a few minutes later, and he led her toward the balcony. When they stepped outside, Virgo was already there. She wondered if he'd been waiting for them, or if it was their nightly routine to look down at the abyss. She offered him a smile, but he didn't return it.

Instead, Virgo was glaring at Vander. "Did you enjoy your meal?" There was a rough edge his words.

"I did. Spending time with *my* mate will always be pleasurable."

"I agree. I took *my* mate for a walk this morning, and we had a pleasurable time."

"I'm aware you went out with *my* mate." Vander moved closer to Virgo as he said the words.

"*My* mate," challenged Virgo. His teeth were bared, and they were practically snarling at each other.

Alarmed, Eva stepped between them before it could escalate. "What are you doing?"

"I'm staking my claim," said Virgo.

"And I'll challenge that claim any day," said Vander, equally intense.

She shook her head. "I'm confused. I thought we were all supposed to be a triad? Is jealousy normal?"

Vander and Virgo both froze for a moment. Virgo even shook his head as Vander took a few deep breaths. "No," said Vander after hesitation.

Virgo nodded. "This definitely isn't normal. We should be fine with sharing, but the idea of him putting his hands on you makes me enraged."

"I feel the same way," said Vander with a snarl in his tone. "I want no one else's hands on you."

She could sense the violence in the air, and she knew it was her fault. It wasn't her fault because of her direct actions, but her presence was causing aggression and conflict between the twins. With a deep breath, she took a step back from between them. "I think the solution is obvious then. I can't see either one of you again. I won't be responsible for tearing you apart, especially when you're supposed to be leading your tribe as a joined unit." She turned away and started walking.

"Wait, Eva, you can't leave me," said Virgo.

She kept walking, heading toward the doors on the balcony that would lead her out of their suite.

"Eva," called Vander behind her. There was a world of agony in his tone, and she almost stumbled to a stop at the naked need. She couldn't do it though. She couldn't choose one over the other, and she certainly couldn't allow them to argue over her and ruin their relationship. The kindest thing she could do for all three of them was to steer clear of Vander and Virgo until she found a way home.

AFTER A LONG AND RESTLESS night, Eva was ready to approach Shiraz again to volunteer to help him find Earth in any way she could. Two pairs of eyes searching the maps had to be better than one, right? Even if he was a little unsettling, he offered her the best chance of getting home.

She set out to find the turret and soon realized she was lost. The fortress was large and intimidating, and it was difficult to remember where everything was located. She must've taken a wrong turn somewhere, because she entered a section she hadn't yet been to. A glimmering aquatic garden caught her attention, and she opened the door to enter it. It was enclosed in what she would call glass, and she imagined the blooms were sensitive. She moved closer, seeing one of the flowers Vander had given her last night. The night's events laid heavily on her heart, and as she stroked a finger across the flower, she wished things could be different.

"Welcome. I don't often get visitors to my private sanctuary." A lower female voice spoke from behind her.

Eva let out a startled gasp and turned to face the woman. She knew she'd seen her before, but she couldn't recall her name at that moment. "Am I not supposed to be here? I can leave."

The woman moved closer, gliding across the room on bare feet. "No, please stay. I've been wanting to speak with you. I'm Feltha, the tribe's shaman. I'm usually the one who finds the matches among our people, but I seem to have had some outside help when it comes to Virgo and Vander." Her eyes gleamed.

Eva was immediately suspicious. "Do you know Freydon Rote?"

Feltha chuckled. "He's a charming creature, isn't he? He came to me for my assistance, assuring me that you were the perfect match for Vander and Virgo. I have a soft spot for those boys, since their mother was my best friend. I immediately agreed to help him in whatever way I could. All I had to do was start the ceremony, and he took care of the rest."

She felt a glimmer of excitement. "Does that mean you can get me home? Do you know how to open a wormhole?"

Feltha shook her head. "I'm afraid that's out of my wheelhouse, Eva. I'm here to guide you on how best to make your bonding work with Virgo and Vander, since I know it's all strange to you."

Eva collapsed onto a chair beside Feltha. "There won't be a bonding. They're arguing over me. I know jealousy isn't normal among twins sharing a mate, and I can't let them be split apart."

Feltha frowned. "It is rather unusual, but I'm confident the solution is simple."

"Oh?" asked Eva guardedly.

"Once you join with them, the aggression will disappear. They'll find harmony with you. Right now, the jealousy and discord are caused by an unconsummated bond. I imagine that would happen with any Drakari pair who didn't have their mate. When a match is identified, consummation takes place, and the union is bonded. You haven't had that yet, and it's causing pain for all three of you."

"I'm not going to join with them. I want to go home and having any kind of relationship with them would just be a complication none of us need."

"The longer you keep them waiting, the worse their aggressions will be, and the deeper the divide."

Eva glared at her she stood up. "I'm not going to be pushed into anything I don't want. Once I'm gone, things will go back to normal for them."

"Will they?" Feltha sighed. "It's almost unheard of in our culture not to accept your mate bond, so I have no idea if the effects will be long-term, but I can't imagine it will improve whether or not you're geographically here. They know of the bond now, and they're both yearning to complete it. Only you can make that happen, so if you find a way home, you might be leaving them in discord. If they can't find unity, they can't lead. Your decisions have ramifications for all of us."

Eva turned away from her. "I was brought here against my will, and whatever consequences happen aren't my doing. I have to do what's best for me, and that's not necessarily what's best for all of you."

Without another word, she turned and walked out of the garden, clinging to the determination to avoid Virgo and Vander so she could find a way home. She ignored the niggle of concern about what would happen to the twins, and perhaps even the entire tribe, if she left their bond unconsummated. That wasn't her problem, and she pushed aside any guilt or worry to focus on an actionable plan to get home.

Chapter 6

IT HAD BEEN TWO DAYS since he'd spoken with Eva. He had seen her in the dining chamber, but that was it. The one time he tried to approach, she had turned and left the room. His only bright spot was knowing she had done the same to Virgo the following morning.

He was full of anger, though he couldn't explain why. He'd never felt so on the edge of violence and out of control before, and it seemed to grow worse by the hour. This must have been how the original Drakari warlords felt. They had been at constant war and probably still were. Only the Sen tampering with their genetics had brought the primal rage under control, but he was barely keeping it in check.

He stared at Eva with a brooding gaze. She was across the chamber from him, with her back obviously facing him. She was speaking to Tarra. Thana was there as well, but she didn't appear to be saying anything. He had very little concern for the other women at the table. Eva consumed him.

He growled when Virgo sat down across from him, blocking his view. "Move."

"No," said Virgo in the same tone. "I don't like you staring at *my* mate that way."

Vander slammed his hand on the table. "She's *my* mate."

"Mine." Virgo's lips skimmed back to reveal his teeth as he practically hissed the word.

Part of Vander was appalled when his arm lifted, and he brought back his hand so he could punch his own brother. Never in a million years could he imagine wanting to inflict harm on his twin, but a darker part of him celebrated when he let his fist fly, smashing into Virgo's temple.

Virgo was quick to respond, leaping across the table and knocking him to the floor. They rolled around, trading punches and insults, until Vander looked up and saw Eva standing over them, hands on her hips, and her lips pursed in disapproval. The fight drained from him, and it must've had a similar effect on Virgo, because he relaxed as well. They rolled away from each other and stood up. On his feet, he was much taller than Eva, yet he somehow felt only inches tall under her gaze.

"I want to talk to both of you. Now." Her tone brooked no argument, and he followed behind her with contrition, as Virgo brought up the rear. Now that the cloud of rage was dissipating, he was shocked and appalled by his behavior. He imagined Virgo was feeling similarly.

She led them to their suite, waiting for one of them to open the door for her, since it was locked. Once Virgo had done so, she stepped inside and then waited for them. She marched over to the arrangement of couches and chairs and pointed at them with a stabbing motion, forefinger extended.

Virgo sat in one chair, and Vander took the one across from him. He couldn't help recalling how he felt as a young man when he had displeased his combat instructor. This was a similar kind of shame. Before she could speak, he looked at Virgo. "I'm sorry. I don't know what came over me."

Virgo nodded. "It's the same for me, brother."

Eva let out a long sigh as she took the couch. She looked at both of them. "I don't like seeing you two fight and tear into each other. I thought avoiding you would make the situation better, but it appears to have just made it worse."

Vander nodded. "The longer I'm without you, the more urgent the need. I can't curb the aggression."

"That's how I feel as well," said Virgo.

"I don't want to be forced to do anything, but I can see staying away from you isn't solving anything. Neither is seeing you individually and increasing your jealousy." Eva's shoulders slumped. "I can't see much choice here."

"We won't have you sacrificing yourself in a mating you don't want," said Vander.

"She never said she didn't want it. She just wants to go home too," said Virgo.

His brother's correction set his teeth on edge, but he managed to rein in the impulse to shout at him. Even now, he could feel the rage starting to bubble to the surface again. "A mate bonding would be for life with us. She clearly doesn't want that."

"She said—"

"I do want you both." Eva's bold admission hung between them all for a moment before she licked her lips. "I do, but if I accept this, I want you both to understand I'm still going home if I get a chance."

Virgo looked wounded. "If we mate, it's for life."

She shrugged a shoulder. "It might be true for your culture, but not for mine. I want to make sure you two aren't constantly fighting, and it seems like securing the bond would be the best way to do that."

Vander shuddered as he got to his feet. "I won't have a mate who martyrs herself. If it's that unpleasant to be with us, you'd be better off steering clear, and we'll find a way to deal with the anger." He stormed away before she could say anything. He heard her calling his name, but Vander kept going, leaving their suites and Virgo and Eva behind him.

Like a raging animal, he prowled through the corridors for a long time, struggling to get a handle on his rage, and to contain his grief. Never had he imagined being matched with a mate who didn't really want him. She was willing to sacrifice herself for the short-term, not realizing how devastated he and Virgo would be if she left after they had joined.

"You look troubled," said Shiraz from behind him.

Vander jumped, startled by Shiraz's unseen arrival, and by the fact he had dropped his guard enough to allow himself to be surprised. He turned to face Barta's nephew. "I'm fine."

"You don't seem fine, Vander. You've been troubled ever since the human came here. It's so unfortunate, after you did so well in the trials." Shiraz sighed. "What I wouldn't have given to be able to compete."

Vander managed to find a shred of sympathy. "It's most unfair that Sereza died, and that you weren't allowed to join the trials."

Shiraz shrugged. "It was a great blow to lose my twin sister, but it makes sense that one of a pair of twins can't participate in the trials. We lead by two or three, and I'm alone." Melancholy bled through his tone.

"It must be rough." Vander was trying to focus on Shiraz, who had only lost Sereza last year. Before that, he'd been training alongside her for the trials. Since Botham's illness had been lingering, the tribe had time to prepare well in advance, knowing they would soon have to replace their Chiefs.

"I think it must be worse to have my twin take my mate."

Vander stiffened. "What?"

Shiraz tipped his head. "I assumed that was what happened? She's not of our culture and doesn't understand our ways. Word is she insisted on choosing between you rather than accepting you both. She's with Virgo now, isn't she?"

Vander could feel the rage stirring again, and he swallowed it down with difficulty as he nodded. "That's not what happened though."

Shiraz smiled. "That's certainly a relief then. I can't imagine how humiliating and enraging it would be to lose a mate to my twin." He bowed his head in a sign of respect. "If you'll excuse me, I have work to do. I'm still trying to find the coordinates for the human's planet, so she can return there. I suspect we'll all be happier with her gone." He chuckled.

Vander curled his hands into fists, struggling to contain his anger. "I can't imagine being happier without her."

"Then I hope you're able to successfully claim her. If you'll excuse me, work calls." With another bow of his head, a gesture traditionally reserved for the acting Chiefs rather than those who had not yet had the Ascension ceremony, he swept past Vander.

Vander stood there, stewing in his own ire. Had walking out given Virgo the opening he'd been looking for? Was his brother even now staking a claim on their mate? The idea sent his blood pounding through his veins, and he rushed back to the suite he shared with his brother.

Chapter 7

EVA WAS CONCERNED ABOUT Vander after his angry departure. She sat on the couch, clutching her hands. Virgo rose from the chair and came to sit beside her, putting his arm around her shoulders. She leaned against him as tears welled. "I handled that badly."

"No, you didn't. It's the rage. I can understand it, because I've been feeling it too. It clouds my mind and distorts my thoughts. Even now, it's pushing me to accept your offer without Vander. It would be wrong to do so, but it's what I want." As he spoke, his other hand settled on her thigh after he brushed aside the *swara*. "I shouldn't be touching you this way. You do want it though, don't you, Eva?" He practically whispered the last words.

His hand trailed slightly up her thigh, and she trembled with desire. His voice permeated her with the essence of temptation, and she swayed closer to him. Virgo kissed her, and she surrendered to his lips and tongue as his hand slid higher, seeking out her throbbing core. The design of the *swara* prevented her from wearing underwear, so he found her bare flesh, swollen with need and dripping with desire. She moaned when his fingers softly traced the line of her mound but didn't yet slip inside. She writhed with need, whimpering.

"Easy, Eva. We have all the time in the world," Virgo said with a chuckle.

She would've glared at him if she could open her eyes. As it was, she was too tense and too focused on what his fingers were doing between her legs to manage any kind of response besides another whimper of need.

Virgo eased a finger inside her, finding ample moisture to ease the progress of his finger as he explored her physiology. "What's this?" He circled her clit as he asked.

"It gives me pleasure," she managed to say in a stuttering tone. It took more strength than she could have imagined to be able to utter even that terse explanation.

"Interesting. Drakari women don't have this. They have something similar inside." As he spoke, he moved his finger down her slit to find her opening. He probed gently, exploring shallowly. "This part's the same."

"Please…" She whimpered the word, feeling on the edge of insanity from the light way he was teasing her.

"How can I refuse such a request?" Virgo stood up, undoing the ties at her shoulder that held the *swara* on before untying the ones on her hips as well. The front of the cloth wafted over her head a moment later as he tossed it backward, and she was bare to him.

Eva reached out her arms, wanting to feel him against her. He took one of her hands and squeezed it as he got to his knees, releasing it before cupping her thighs to splay them so he could look at her. She trembled under his unwavering gaze, feeling naked and helpless, yet conversely cherished and protected. There was such tenderness in his gaze, though his hunger was clear as well.

"It wouldn't be right to claim you without Vander, but I can pleasure you. Would you like that, Eva?"

She nodded frantically, knowing she should probably insist on waiting for Vander for any activities, but unable to resist the lure of what Virgo was offering.

He used one of his hands to part her folds so he could look closer. He made a sound that was difficult to interpret, but it sounded like anticipation.

She whimpered when two fingers from his other hand started stroking her clit, seeming to know he had to be gentle even though he had no experience with clitorises. He appeared to know just the spots to stroke, and her hips leapt off the couch. He found the most sensitive spot, and she could feel herself building to an orgasm as he started to stroke lightly. She groaned in protest when his fingers slipped lower, once more finding her opening. He surged inside, carefully probing each inch of her.

"You're so tight."

She whimpered. "I haven't done this before." None of the humans or cyborgs had caught her attention enough for her to be willing to share her body with them. She wondered now, with her defenses lowered, if she'd been unconsciously waiting for this moment and this man—these men.

Even now, she could feel a void. There was certainly something missing, and she knew it was Vander. She wanted to do the honorable thing and tell Virgo to stop until they spoke with Vander again, but then he bent his head, and his tongue slipped along her slit, and she was lost. All nobility faded, and she focused solely on coming.

Eva threw back her head and closed her eyes, a prisoner to the sensations shooting through her. He put his hands under her buttocks to adjust her position, and then his tongue and face were even closer to her. His nose edged against her clit in rhythm while his tongue explored her folds and entrance.

Her body was awash with sensation, and she was having trouble separating what she was feeling so she could identify it. All she knew was she was close to coming, and when Virgo put his hands on her breasts and tugged lightly at the nipples, it sent her over the edge. She shouted her pleasure and collapsed against the couch, eyes closed as she trembled.

It was only as the pleasure started to fade that she realized Virgo's hands were still on her buttocks, and there were two hands covering her breasts. She opened her eyes and looked up, surprised and yet unsurprised to find Vander had joined them. She licked her lips and struggled to speak. All she could manage was to croak his name.

His smile was tender, and his expression appeared untroubled. "I came back to stop you from joining with Virgo, but when I saw you like this, in such a natural state of passion, I couldn't stop myself from joining. Is that all right?"

She nodded, reaching up for him. He was standing behind the couch, so when he kissed her, his mouth was upside down to hers. His hair fell across her torso and face, but she paid it little attention. She reached up to cup his face, bringing his mouth more solidly against her before gasping.

Virgo's tongue had started squirming around again inside her, and she whimpered from the throbbing it elicited. Virgo laughed against her, which sent vibrations through her core that made her stomach clench. She gasped his name, but it was swallowed by Vander's mouth.

A moment later, Vander lifted his head, and she loosened her hands from around his face as he stood up. She was bereft without him, though it was difficult to focus on anything besides Vander's tongue.

"It's my turn, brother."

Eva tensed as she waited to see if Virgo would surrender his spot between her thighs. After a hesitation, he stood up and backed away so Vander could take his place. Virgo came to where Vander had been, loosening his waistband and pulling out the long girth of his cock. It was a slightly paler green than the rest of him, but the size was what caught her attention more than the shade. He looked similar to what she knew of human physiology, but bigger.

When he brushed his erection against her cheek, she turned her head and extended her tongue to taste him. He was sweet and salty, though his semen was thinner than she had seen in her limited experience, which consisted of giving a hand job to a boy around her age a few years ago. She'd had no interest in sleeping with him, and he'd found another girl who would.

Vander's tongue surged inside her at the same time Virgo started to fill her mouth with his cock. She tried to relax and accept it, barely able to fit it between her lips. She let Virgo set the pace, since she had no experience, and she could barely move her mouth. All she could do was suck in her cheeks to give him more suction as he thrust in and out of her.

"I need you," said Vander.

Eva couldn't turn her head to look at him or respond verbally, so she lifted her thighs higher to wrap around him, hoping he understood she was giving him permission.

She was afraid, trembling slightly, as she heard Vander's pants hit the floor. If he was as large as his brother, she was afraid it would hurt when he entered her for the first time, but she wanted him more than she could say. She wanted both of them with a soul-consuming need she couldn't have verbalized, even if she didn't have Virgo's cock in her mouth.

Vander's shaft rested against her opening, and she tried to relax as he spread her thighs even wider and held open her lips with his thumbs. His cock eased inside, and she stiffened slightly. He was definitely as big as his brother.

"Stroke her clit. She seems to like that." Virgo offered the advice in a tone that was broken and filled with harsh breathing.

"The little nub?" asked Vander.

Eva assumed Virgo must have nodded or responded nonverbally, because Vander stroked her clit seconds later. He brought her to the edge of coming again, where she was barely noticing the girth of his cock, before he ventured deeper inside her. He pushed through her barrier with one painful thrust that made her whimper, but as he increased the pace of his stroking, the pain soon faded.

She creamed against him as Vander thrust in and out of her while Virgo mimicked his rhythm in her mouth. Eva was at the mercy of their passions, unable to do much besides endure their forceful technique. It was the most amazing thing, and she only wanted more.

Virgo came in her mouth a moment later, letting out a sound that was pure primal satisfaction as he spilled his seed down her throat. From her angle, she was able to swallow it all, and when he pulled his cock from her mouth, she instinctively protested. She wanted him inside her.

"She's like heaven," said Vander, clearly speaking to Virgo.

"I look forward to finding out."

Eva glanced at Virgo's cock, surprised to see he was already erect again. "Is that normal stamina for your people?" Her jaw was pleasantly sore when she spoke.

Virgo grinned. "Especially for a newly mated male."

"I'm not sure I can survive much more," said Eva with an awkward chuckle. They broke off into silence as Vander found the magical spot on her clit that brought her the most pleasure. He focused on stroking it while thrusting inside her, and she came a moment later, just as the first spurts of his seed filled her as well. She clenched her thighs around him, needing an anchor to keep her from flying off into the stars, and Virgo grasped both her hands as though providing support.

The climax ravished her, and she collapsed against the sofa in a boneless heap a moment later. She was only vaguely aware of Virgo lifting and carrying her to the stairs and downward. Vander followed behind, and she soon found herself lying on the bed. She opened her eyes, smiling up at the twins, who were perched on either side of her. She lifted her hands and cupped one of each of their cheeks, rubbing lightly with her thumb. "I never expected anything like this."

"We aren't done yet, unless you need a break," said Virgo with a hint of warning.

She shook her head. "I think I could die happy doing this."

"You'll live happily for years and years with us," said Vander with a snarl. He clearly didn't like her phrasing.

She didn't bother to explain to him that it was a saying rather than something she was serious about. She also didn't call him on the fact that he was referring to years and years when she still intended to return home to Earth if she had the chance. It wasn't worth arguing about it now and ruining their moment.

For their talk of not being done, she was surprised when they both left her a moment later. She moaned to protest but couldn't form words. Instead, she snuggled against the pillow and laid on her side, feeling a hint of exhaustion starting to creep in. It was probably normal after such an intense physical experience.

Virgo was the first to return to her, lying in front of her. He positioned her so that her thigh was splayed over his, and his cock slowly eased inside her. She was still wet and excited, so he had little difficulty filling her sheath. She clung to him, surprised when he didn't start to thrust.

The bed behind her dipped as Vander joined them, and she stiffened a moment later as she felt something cool and soft, yet slightly slick, brushing against her backside. It was his finger coated with something, and she let out a sound of uncertainty as his digit breached her puckered hole, soothing in its passage. She expected pain, but there was only a slight tingling sensation as his finger moved deeper inside her. "What's on your hand?"

"Just a blend of herbs and flowers that will ensure you have no discomfort while we both claim you."

Vander's explanation made her eyes widen as she realized his intent. They were both going to be inside her at the same time. She should've realized that, but she had no experience with threesomes, and it hadn't occurred to her. She was afraid, yet curious and excited.

"Is this what you want?" asked Virgo, still unmoving inside her pussy.

After a moment, she nodded. "Yes, I think it is." His finger didn't hurt as it entered her, and neither did a second one when it joined the first. Whatever he was rubbing inside her had the desired effect, and she relaxed even when she felt the head of his cock pressing against her pucker a moment later. Eva took a deep breath as Vander gently pushed his way inside her. He didn't rush her, taking only an inch or so at a time, until she was fully accommodating his girth.

She felt overstuffed and on the verge of pain. With both men inside her, she was afraid they might tear her apart, but she couldn't deny it felt good, even though neither one of them were moving yet

"How are you feeling?" asked Virgo.

She met his gaze. "Good. I think I want more."

Vander and Virgo started to move, and they were doing most of the work. They set the pace between them, finding a naturally matching rhythm that managed to stimulate her completely.

Her world distilled down to the two shafts inside her and the two men holding her between them. She put one hand behind her to cup Vander's hip and lifted the other one to clench Virgo's shoulder. Though she couldn't see Vander, she could feel the bond with him just as strong as it was with Virgo.

The way they moved inside her hit all the best places, and she didn't require extra stimulation to her clit. It seemed like only seconds after they began that she reached orgasm. She shouted her pleasure, and her voice sounded hoarse to her own ears as she exploded around them, before collapsing onto the bed.

They kept going, clearly not ready to come yet. She wondered if she was going to survive the extent of their passions, but she didn't protest. She simply surrendered to the motions and the orgasms that kept coming until what seemed like many minutes later, when Vander finally surrendered his control and came in her backside. Virgo followed seconds later inside her, and they fell into an exhausted heap.

She fell asleep almost immediately, though they woke her several times throughout the night, sometimes with Vander inside her sheath while Virgo was behind her, and other times the other way. By the time they seemed sated, she was completely exhausted, but she'd never known such pleasure, and she regretted nothing as she fell asleep for the final time that night between them before waking hours later alone.

Chapter 8

IT MUST'VE BEEN OBVIOUS to everyone living in the fortress that she and Vander and Virgo had bonded. She could tell by the knowing smiles and giggles from some of the younger Drakari women. She was a little embarrassed to walk among them, especially since the *swara* revealed every love bite and passionate bruise on her legs and thighs and up the side of her body. She had a particularly large hickey on her neck, but none of the clothing in her closet had provided any better coverage than the *swara* she had reclaimed from the sofa in their suite before going to her own room to bathe and change.

She could feel herself flushing as she approached the table where Thana and Tarra sat. Tarra grinned at her with a wink, and Thana glowered in her direction. As she sat down, Tarra asked, "Would you like to come to the surface with us? We're going to gather *klavits.*"

"What's a *klavit*?"

"Those," said Tarra, pointing to one of the clumps of food on her plate.

They were a favorite of Eva's, and she looked forward to being out of the water. Regardless of what they planned to harvest—even moth-lace, though the concept of drinking insect webs still unsettled her—she would've been up for going along. It also couldn't hurt to get out of the fortress and away from all the knowing gazes for a while.

"Have you seen Virgo and Vander?" asked Eva.

"Perhaps they've come to their senses and are avoiding you," said Thana sourly.

Eva ignored her, looking at Tarra.

Tarra shook her head. "I haven't, but they're probably preparing for the Ascension ceremony. There's some ritual they have to memorize or something. There's usually a week or two of preparation. Now that you're bonded, that's the next logical step."

Eva frowned. "Can they not ascend without a mate?"

"I'm sure they could, but it's never been done before. There is a certain order of events that take place. One's mate is usually selected earlier in life than Virgo and Vander opted for. They were busy preparing for the trials and chose to wait on the mating ceremony."

Eva considered that a good thing. If they had asked for their mate a few years ago, she would've either been too young, or she might've been too weak and naïve to be able to stand up for herself to two such strong, dominant men.

After they'd finished eating, the three of them headed for the surface. It still felt strange to Eva to swim once they were out of the fortress and in the open ocean. It was starting to feel more comfortable and natural, but there were quite a few moments that still jarred her and reminded her exactly where she was and how she was living now.

They emerged at the surface without incident, and once they were on one of the crystals, Eva asked, "Are there predators we have to worry about in the ocean?" It was a belated thought, and she wished she'd asked it earlier.

"There're a few, but they're usually farther away from the fortress. They don't come around the area much. I suspect they've learned to fear the Sen defensive measures around the fortress as much as we fear the predators."

"How will I know what's dangerous?"

Thana let out a laugh that wasn't entirely kind. "If it's large and has vicious teeth that are trying to eat you, I'd suggest you swim away."

Eva rolled her eyes, though she supposed that was probably good advice, even if a bit vague. "How do we find the *klavits*?"

"They like to burrow under the crystals, so I need to move those aside." Tarra demonstrated by standing up from the one she was on and lugging it slightly upright and over to the side. As she did so, Eva saw little legs kicking in the sand as they tried to burrow deeper. Tarra scooped them up and placed them in a mesh bag she'd brought along. "It's a simple as that." As she spoke, she handed Eva another bag. Thana already had one of her own.

They spent the day working their way around the beach, moving the crystals to gather as many *klavits* as possible. Gradually, they worked their way higher up the cliffside, finding all the nooks and crannies where the *klavits* like to hide.

They'd come at least twenty-five feet upward from the beach when Eva found herself on the same crystal jutting out from the rockface as Thana. It was a wide crystal, but she was still nervous. It took her a moment to realize why—she was afraid Thana would try to push her off the crystal and be done with her. Clearly, the other woman still didn't like her.

Feeling tense, Eva decided to go to a different crystal. She backed away and slid down the rockface, taking the one below. She was bent down to scoop into the crevices where the crystal joined the rockface when she heard a cry. She looked up in time to see Thana scrambling to hold on to the crystal as she slid off the edge. It was smooth and slippery and provided little purchase.

Eva glanced down reflexively, finding they were above a collection of crystals on the rocky beach below. If she couldn't catch and hold Thana, they would both hit the rocks rather than water. She had a split second to decide whether she wanted to let Thana fall, or if she wanted to try to save her at the risk of her own life.

Even as she was thinking about it, she reached out and grabbed Thana's hand, just barely grasping it before it was out of her reach. She braced herself for the jolt as Thana's arrested fall shot through her. Locking her legs around the crystal, which was thinner than the one she'd been on with Thana, she managed to hold on somehow. Her shoulder ached, and she could feel it pop out of the joint as Thana dangled below her. She cried out in agony at the feel, but she didn't let go.

Tarra was making her way to them as quickly as possible, and Eva was focusing on her, hoping she got to them in time. It was a shock when she heard Vander call from below her. "Let go. We'll catch her."

Eva couldn't look down, not in her position, so she had to trust them. Thana whimpered a little as she let go of her hand, but Eva did so, trusting in her mates. She heard a grunt a moment later, and it sounded like the impact of her body against another. She wanted to cling to the crystal, but she couldn't get her arm up with her shoulder out of place. "I'm stuck," she said to Tarra as she reached her.

"Let go," said Vander.

They had clearly caught Thana, but it was easier to let go of someone else than it was to let go of her own perch. Still, she trusted them to catch her, so she loosened her thighs from around the crystal and let the arm she'd been clutching with so tightly relax as well.

A second later, she was falling, and she screamed in reaction. What felt like hours later, but was only seconds, she landed safely in Virgo and Vander's arms. They stumbled under the brunt of catching her, but they didn't fall. They just held her, probably tighter than necessary, as they both kissed her exposed face.

She would've kissed them back, except her shoulder was killing her. "I'm in pain. Please put me down."

They immediately did so, and their hands ran all over her body, looking for injuries.

"It's my shoulder," she said as she locked gazes with Thana. The woman was standing on her own two feet but hugging herself. She was trembling, and when Tarra worked her way down the rockface and joined them a moment later, Thana turned to embrace her twin and sob.

"What are you doing here?" asked Tarra, though she looked as relieved as Eva felt at their unexpected arrival.

"We both sensed Eva's fear, so we swam as hard as we could. We just knew where to find her." Virgo looked surprised.

Vander didn't seem as surprised. "The stronger the mating bond, the more connected we are."

Eva didn't have a clear explanation for how it could work, but it clearly had. They'd sensed she was afraid, and they'd come for her without hesitation. She admired how they could listen so unquestioningly to their instincts, and she was grateful they'd done so, or the outcome would have been very different.

After a few minutes, Thana had calmed down enough to return to the fortress, and Eva was feeling calmer as well. Her mates had her between them, and they were doing most of the swimming for her after they all jumped into the water. They took her directly to Feltha, and Eva learned she was also the healer.

After looking at her shoulder for a moment, Feltha nodded. "Let me get you something for the pain so we can put it back in place. Vander and Virgo, you'll want to stick nearby, because I might need you to hold her down."

"I'm not sure I want to do this," said Eva.

"You have to," said Virgo, squeezing the hand of the arm that wasn't injured.

She nodded, knowing there was no way around it. Feltha returned a moment later with something that was dark-green and foul-smelling. With a grimace, Eva chugged it all before handing it back. "Now what?"

"We give it a few minutes for the pain relief properties to take effect, and then we'll return the shoulder to its proper alignment." Feltha didn't blink.

"Don't you have some advanced Sen technology that could do that?"

"We have the facilities, but it's one of the areas we still don't fully understand how to use completely. What we do know has been learned through experimentation, and I don't think you'd want to volunteer for an experiment when this is something I can handle, do you?" Feltha asked with a sparkle in her eyes.

Eva reluctantly shook her head. She wasn't eager to have Feltha popping her shoulder back into place, but nor was she ready to go lie down in some alien equipment and let them try to figure out how to fix her with random presses of buttons or something.

A few minutes later, Virgo and Vander held her while Feltha gripped her shoulder. There was a brief, agonizing moment when she popped the shoulder back into the socket, but then it felt better almost immediately. It still hurt, and there would be some throbbing pain for a while, according to Feltha, but the worst was over.

"Take her to your suite and let her rest." Feltha shook her finger at her mates. "I mean rest for at least the next twelve hours. I know how it is to be newly mated, but she needs to make sure her shoulder stays in place."

"We would never do anything to harm her." Vander sounded outraged at the idea.

"We'll see that she rests and gets everything she needs," said Virgo, sounding slightly calmer.

Feltha nodded her satisfaction before taking Eva's hand to hold between her wrinkled fingers. "Rest and let them take care of you. That's their job."

Eva nodded, in no mood to argue with anyone. All she wanted to do was sleep, and she suspected there'd been something in the drink Feltha made her that initiated the response. It had been more than a pain reliever, she was sure.

They carried her between them, though she could've walked. They'd squabbled over who would carry her for a moment, but Eva had spoken up and told them both to do it. That seemed the easiest way to solve the dispute, so she let them carry her to their rooms, and they returned her to the bed where she'd found such amazing pleasure the night before.

Even in pain, and with the undeniable urge to sleep pressing upon her, she could feel a stir of arousal at the memories. It wasn't enough to keep her awake or fight off the effects of the drink Feltha gave her, and her eyelids closed seconds later.

Chapter 9

"THE ASCENSION CEREMONY is tomorrow night," said Virgo as he rubbed her feet.

"You'll have a part to play as well," said Vander, who was lying behind her with his hand over her midriff.

Eva stirred herself from her passionate daze as she realized that meant she had been here almost a month. In some ways, that seemed impossible. She must've fallen into a pattern of behavior, and while she hadn't given up on being able to go home to Earth, it hadn't seemed such a prominent goal each day since she'd become lovers with Vander and Virgo. "What kind of role?" She tried to hide the fear from her voice. She knew they had been preparing for the ceremony along with their other duties, yet she'd had no chance to practice anything.

"You'll stand there with us and agree to the oath Barta will issue you." Vander made it sound easy.

She frowned and met Virgo's gaze, unable to hide her dismay. "You've been preparing for weeks. Why don't I have a run-through as well?"

Virgo blinked. "Oh, the ceremony for us is essentially the same. Most of our preparation has been to take over for Barta after the ceremony. She's been training us on the inside details of being the Chiefs."

Eva let out a ragged exhale. "Oh. I thought you'd spent all those hours preparing for the ceremony itself." Relief swept through her, quickly followed by dread. If she accepted her role as their mates and took some oath, it had a permanent feel about it. If she managed to find a way home, leaving would violate her oath.

Could she take the oath while harboring the idea of leaving in good conscience? It seemed wrong to take an oath she might not keep, but her mates would be disappointed if she didn't.

That she referred to them as her mates worried her. She had been trying to keep it on a more casual, temporary basis. She wanted to be able to walk away if the option presented itself, but she was suddenly uncertain she could do so. She remained unconvinced about taking the oath as well though. She needed to figure out what was best for her and try to remove emotions from the equation.

VANDER AND VIRGO HAD disappeared to Barta's chamber again, so she joined Thana and Tarra for breakfast. Thana had continued to be nicer to her after she'd saved her life, so she broached the subject with both of them. "What's entailed for the Chiefs' wife during the Ascension ceremony?"

"It could be the Chiefs' husband or husbands as well," said Thana as she bit into a *nari* fruit harvested from the surface. Eva had discovered a taste for them as well.

"Women can ascend too?" As she asked the question, she realized how stupid it was. The current Chief was a woman, only being replaced because her twin brother had died. She shook her head. "Never mind. "

"I only vaguely remember the last ceremony," said Tarra.

"We were about six then," said Thana.

"I think she just stood there. Only Botham was mated at the time. At the end of the ceremony, the retiring Chief asked her to swear to support the Chiefs and maintain loyalty to the tribe. I think." Tarra frowned, clearly concentrating.

"I think I remember she just said two words or so for the whole ceremony." Thana put aside the *nari* fruit stone.

"It doesn't sound too bad." Except the part where she was swearing to support her mates and remain loyal to the tribe. It was a clear conflict with her intended goal of returning home. She nibbled on her lip as she considered the circumstances, coupled with the reality of actually being able to return home.

As though to add to her confusion, Shiraz suddenly appeared beside the table. He inclined his head respectfully toward the three of them. Then his gaze focused on Eva. "I found Earth."

Her heart leapt with excitement, and she was out of her seat without thought. "Show me, please."

He nodded his head and turned away to lead her from the dining room. They climbed the same amount of stairs as before, which gave her time to start thinking. Was she really going to go through the wormhole right now without saying goodbye to Vander and Virgo? That didn't feel right, so she assured herself she wouldn't be departing just yet. There were people she would have to say goodbye to, including Vander and Virgo. That thought sent a wrench through her chest, and she rubbed it absentmindedly, as though that would relieve heartache.

They reached the turret a few minutes later, and he led her inside. He took her to equipment that had previously been deactivated. She could see flashes of light and what might've been vegetation, but it was all basically a blur. "How do you know it's Earth?"

"I've been working day and night on this so you could return home. I'm positive." He spoke passionately.

"That's great, but I'm sorry you spent so much time on it."

He turned to frown at her. "Your goal was to get home, and my goal was to help you before the Ascension ceremony. It's worked out perfectly."

She frowned. Was he recognizing the same issue that she was—committing to the oath meant she would stay, or she would end up betraying it? "You must care a lot about the tribe."

He nodded. "Of course I do. I would've competed for the trials if it hadn't been for an arcane rule that prevents only one from competing unless they're a singleton. My sister's death ruined my hopes."

He looked shattered, and she moved in a little closer to pat him awkwardly on the shoulder. "I'm sorry. That must be very difficult."

He glared up at her, though his anger didn't seem to be directed her way. "It's even more difficult to see Virgo and Vander ascend." Naked hatred shown in his expression.

She took a step back instinctively. "I see. Well, I need to tell them goodbye before I leave. Thank you for finding my way home."

He glared at her. "The wormhole is unstable, and it won't stay open for long. You have to leave now."

Her options were distilled down to that moment. She could leave now to return to her life on Earth, but that would mean leaving Virgo and Vander. "Can you reopen it if I want to come back for a visit?"

He shook his head. "It's a one-way trip." His tone made it ambiguous whether it was impossible to reopen the wormhole, or if he just refused to do so.

"Why don't you like Virgo and Vander?" she asked to buy herself some time to decide.

Shiraz frowned. "I don't dislike them."

For some reason, that sent relief spiraling through her. She started to smile and apologize for her misunderstanding.

"I hate them both. I loathe them. I never liked either of them from the time we were little. They were favored because they were strong and bold. Teachers preferred them, all the adults and everyone loved them, including Aunt Barta and Uncle Botham. There was clear favoritism from the Chiefs, and it was common knowledge that Vander and Virgo were their preferred choice for ascending after them someday."

"So you didn't like them because they were popular? That seems a harsh reason to hate them."

His lips skinned back from his teeth as he practically spat out, "You don't know my reasons."

She was trying to coax them from him, wanting a more complete picture of the situation. "Were they mean to you?"

Shiraz laughed, but it was a cold sound. "Of course they weren't. Vander and Virgo were practically perfect. They are kind to everyone, and they were the first to stick up for anyone who was being teased. They rescued me more than once. Do you know how humiliating that is?"

She shook her head, confused by his words. "I'm not really sure why you don't like them. I guess it doesn't matter."

His hands clenched into fists as he exploded from his chair. "It matters. Do you know how many times my parents held up Vander and Virgo as an example of what I should be doing? My academic achievements meant nothing to them. They wanted me to be more like Virgo and Vander."

"That must've been rough. I can see why you would resent them if your parents were doing that, but it wasn't Virgo and Vander's fault."

"Nothing was ever their fault, including Sereza's death." He shouted the words at her.

Eva took another step back. "Are you saying that Vander and Virgo had something to do with your sister's death?"

Shiraz sneered at her. "The silly fool had her heart set on being the mate to one of them. She was in love with both, so she'd sneak around and follow them so she could stare at them like a lovesick idiot. They probably knew and didn't want to hurt her feelings by discouraging her." He made that sound like it was the worst action in the world they could do, rather than one of kindness.

"One day, she followed them out for training in the open ocean. I think they were working on stealth or something, along with Botham. The silly idiot tried to hide herself, and she ended up among a nest of *saard*. She was stung multiple times, but the spine of one would've been enough to kill her. When she died, she took all chance with her of me competing in the trial."

She noted he didn't sound heartbroken that his sister had died. He just sounded angry and bitter that he'd lost his chance because of her death.

"How long will the wormhole remain stable?"

He shrugged. "Likely a matter of minutes, so you need to go through now."

It was down to this moment, and she had to make a hard decision. Earth and her family there, or Virgo and Vander? Even as she started to contemplate it, the pang in her chest told her the answer. She couldn't leave Virgo and Vander. She'd fallen in love with them, and they seemed to feel the same way about her. She'd be giving up a lifetime of happiness and pleasure in their arms to return to the familiar.

The idea of never seeing her parents, siblings, and friends at least once more cut through her, but it wasn't nearly the same level of grief and pain as it was to imagine never seeing Virgo and Vander again. Much as she hated to admit it, Freydon Rote must've been correct. This was where she belonged, and with the two men who cherished her.

She cleared her throat. "I guess, in that case, I'm going to have to stay here. If there's only one chance to go, and I can't return, I can't go. I want to be with Virgo and Vander. I'm sorry you worked so hard on this, but I can't leave."

Shiraz covered the distance between them in what felt like seconds, grabbing her arm and jerking her forward. "You can, and you will. If you leave before the ceremony, those two buffoons will fall apart. They'll finally know what it's like to lose, and they won't be able to proceed. You're the key to destroying them."

She started fighting back, digging in her heels and screaming as loudly as she could, hoping Vander and Virgo could sense her fear. She was closer to them in the fortress than she'd been on the surface, so surely they could. Would they reach her in time though?

He just laughed in her face. "By the time anyone gets here, you'll be through the wormhole. Would you like to know a secret?" he asked in a sinister fashion.

She shook her head.

"Too bad. I have no idea where the wormhole opens. I finally managed to get the technology up and running. I've known how to use the plotting system, but not the actual wormholes, but now I've generated one. It could be anywhere, but it doesn't matter...to me. All that matters is having you off Senufo."

She continued to fight against him as he got closer to the wormhole generator. She could see a little better through the screen, and she gasped when a large creature went by. She could only see its leg and part of the spines extending from it, but it was enough to tell her it certainly wasn't Earth. "You can't do this."

He wrapped his hand around her throat. He wasn't as large as many of the other Drakari, but he was still bigger and stronger than her. "Each tear they cry in mourning will make me laugh with pleasure." As he spoke, his hand tightened around her throat.

She grabbed his hand with both of hers, trying to loosen his grasp. She managed to get two fingers to loosen, which marginally improved her flow of oxygen. At least she wasn't on the verge of passing out now, and she kicked him as hard as she could in the groin. The fact that he was holding her by her throat actually offered her an advantage in the situation, because it brought her foot that much closer and gave him less time to block.

His hand relaxed around her throat, and she fell to the floor as he let out a hissing sound and cupped his anatomy. He was so close to the wormhole that when he staggered backward, he started to get sucked in. She let out a cry as he reached forward and grabbed hold of her leg, clearly intending to drag her through with him. She screamed again, doing her best to get away from his grip as the door burst open.

All she saw were Virgo and Vander, but she knew others were there as well. Vander immediately grabbed her, and Virgo pried Shiraz's hand from her calf as her foot neared the wormhole. It sucked Shiraz through seconds later, and then the machine shut down.

"Are you okay?" Virgo sounded frantic.

She nodded, but was distracted from answering as Barta moved closer, grief visible in her expression.

"What happened?"

Eva remembered again that Shiraz was Barta's nephew. She swallowed the lump in her throat and explained as best she could. When she'd finished, she held her breath while she waited to see if Barta would hold her accountable for Shiraz's disappearance.

The Chief looked stoic, and she nodded just once. "He was always a troubled boy, but I'd hoped he would outgrow it as he became a man. I always encouraged him to emulate Virgo and Vander, but he never did."

Eva didn't tell Barta that her encouragement to be like Vander and Virgo had fueled Shiraz's hatred for them and his determination to get revenge for perceived slights. That would only make the older woman feel worse. Instead, she said a simple, "I'm sorry."

Barta nodded and turned away, tears visible on her cheeks in that brief moment before her back was to Eva.

"Let's get you out of here," said Vander. As he spoke, he lifted her into his arms. Virgo was right beside her as they took her from Shiraz's turret and down the stairs. Her mates took her straight to their suite and the bed they all shared now, seeming to need to reassure themselves she was all right in there. She was happy to surrender to their desperate lovemaking, because she needed the closeness as well.

Chapter 10

THE FOLLOWING NIGHT, she stood on the dais between Vander and Virgo as Feltha stood in front of them a few steps below. Barta was already finished with her severing ceremony, and she stood in the crowd with the others, looking composed, though her eyes still appeared puffy. Eva had learned from her mates the previous evening that Shiraz and Sereza had been Barta's unofficial heirs, since she'd never produced offspring. It would be a long time before Barta smiled again, having lost both of her adopted children.

Eva was forced to concentrate and stop thinking sympathetic thoughts for Barta when Feltha's gaze focused on her. Feltha seemed to see all her uncertainty and doubt, and there was almost an air of challenge when she started speaking the oath. As she finished, she said, "Do you accept your role and your burdens?"

It was the moment of truth, and she had little hesitation when she said, "Yes." She'd already decided yesterday to stay with Vander and Virgo, and though the wormhole hadn't turned out to be to Earth, it had helped her clarify what was important, and where she belonged.

After that, it turned into a big party, and she ate and danced and drank along with everyone else, until she was feeling pleasantly tipsy. Vander and Virgo still appeared mostly sober, and she watched them with pleasure, enjoying her place in their life, though she missed her family terribly.

She stumbled over to take a seat, still watching them, but feeling less like she might fall. She'd definitely overindulged in the fermented *nari* fruit punch. She couldn't take her eyes off them as they danced together, along with several other Drakari in a traditional dance. She let out a happy sigh, already imagining the night ahead of them.

"I'm not one to say I told you so, but I did know what I was talking about, dear Eva."

She let out a startled bleat at the words and turned to look beside her, seeing Freydon Rote seated on the bench she was occupying. He was smiling at her, though his mouth part hadn't formed. She could just see in his eyes that he was beaming.

He still wasn't her favorite person, and she glared at him. "I'm surprised to see you show your face around here. I thought you were done meddling."

He shook his head. "You're such a strong mix of your mother and father. I'm not surprised you still harbor me ill-will, but I've come for something you'll like."

She eyed him warily, still not trusting the gelatinous peach blob. "I'll believe that when I see it."

"May I have your pendant?"

She wrapped her hand around it automatically, withdrawing slightly. "No."

Freydon tilted his head slightly, somehow managing to convey his exasperation even without most of his features visible, aside from his eyes. "Come now. I'll give it right back."

Hesitantly, she slipped it off and handed it over, nervous when she no longer maintained grip on any part of it. "I want it back."

"And you shall have it back." He touched it, and it glowed faintly for a moment before he handed it back to her. "You now have a way home back to Earth and the time you came from. That way, you can visit your family, and they can visit you—though I suggest they bring SCUBA equipment to get to the fortress, since none of the Grecopans, humans, or cyborgs will have gills." He laughed.

She stared at it. "How does it work?" She hardly dared to believe what he was telling her. "You said I was stuck here, and I'd have to adapt."

He waved a hand. "That was just a little fib, Eva. I knew you needed to find your groove here and decide to stay. Now that you've accepted you belong with Vander and Virgo, it's safe enough to give you passage home so you can visit. Or should I say to Earth, because Senufo is now your home, isn't it?" His eyes sparkled, and he clearly enjoyed being right.

She grudgingly nodded. "You still didn't tell me how it works."

"It's simple. Just press your thumb to the heart of the figure, and the wormhole will open."

Eva did so, and there were gasps of shock all around her as a glimmering circle opened a few feet in front of her. "Now what?"

"You'd walk through when you're ready to visit. As soon as you want to close it, just touch the heart again."

Since she wasn't ready to visit yet, she did that. "Am I the only one who can work the wormhole, or do they have a way on the Earth side too?"

Freydon looked regretful. "I'm afraid you're the only one who can open and close it." He leaned a little closer, lowering his voice slightly, "I'm not really supposed to give anyone the ability to move through time and space, even on a fixed coordinate like this, so shush." He pressed his finger to his mouth part that appeared a second before the digit reached it.

"How will they get hold of me if they need me?"

He shrugged a loosely formed shoulder. "I assume you can set up some system with them, or perhaps open the wormhole every day. You're a smart girl, and you'll figure it out."

"Thanks." She still didn't sound all that grateful, and she softened her tone when she realized. "Thank you for bringing me Vander and Virgo, or should I say bringing me to Vander and Virgo? You're a sly little alien, Freydon, and I don't trust you any farther than I can throw you." She winked at him as she said the words.

He laughed, clearly delighted. "Perhaps that's for the best, but you should know I have only the best intentions for you and your mates. I just want you all to be happy. Your mother's one of my favorite matches, along with sweet Penny. I wanted to make sure her daughter was equally happy."

She softened toward Freydon in that moment, blinking away tears. "That's kind of you, Freydon. I don't necessarily approve of your methods, but I thank you for what you've done for me."

He nodded his head. "You'll be searching for a purpose, so I ensured you could read Sen, by the way. There are tomes of knowledge that await unlocking."

Her eyes widened. "You think I should become a librarian?" It sounded exotic compared to the future she'd always thought she'd have, doing manual labor to reclaim Earth.

He nodded once. "You'll be good at it."

"Will you be coming back, Freydon?" Eva held her breath, not certain if she wanted to see him again or not.

He let out a regretful sigh. "I don't expect to see you again, dear Eva, but I know you and your mates will be happy. May I suggest you name the little one Freydon?"

She frowned. "I don't know what you mean."

His gaze moved to her stomach. He nodded meaningfully. "You're going to find out yourself in a few days, so I'm just hastening the timeline." He winked at her. "Freydon does have a nice ring to it, don't you think?"

As she realized what he was telling her, her mouth dropped open. "I'm pregnant?" At his delighted grin, she felt her lips moving upright until she was smiling hard enough to hurt her cheeks. "Thank you."

Freydon chuckled again. "I had little to do with that aspect, but I've always liked the name Freydon." He winked at her again.

She shook her head, smiling back at him. "Thank you, Freydon." She reached out to touch the closest part of his blobby body. "I might've been wrong about you."

"Those are probably the kindest words you've ever said to me." With a deep belly laugh, Freydon disappeared.

She looked up, realizing Vander and Virgo had witnessed most of the exchange with Freydon. For that matter, everyone attending the ceremony—which was pretty much the whole tribe aside from the ill or infirm—had seen most of the exchange.

"We're pregnant," said Virgo with excitement as he swept forward and lifted her into his arms to swing her around. Vander had his arms around her as well, and they both held her against them.

"We have a new reason to celebrate," said Feltha, and the party got underway again with even more frantic pursuit of fun and joy.

"Did you hear the part about the wormhole?" she asked when Virgo and Vander gave her a little room to breathe.

They both nodded. "Will you be returning to Earth?" Vander seemed to be preparing himself for the possibility.

She nodded, seeing Vander and Virgo both frown. "For visits. I'd like you to come with me to meet my parents. They'll be worried sick, but once they hear what Freydon's done, I imagine they'll forgive him. They really like the little peach trickster for some reason." She sounded harsh, but she couldn't deny she now had a soft spot for Freydon as well.

"We would be honored to meet your family, just as we're honored to know our children grow inside you." Virgo spoke with intensity as his hand cupped her stomach. "Will they be boys or girls or both?" He wasn't really asking her. It was clearly a rhetorical question uttered from his complete sense of awe.

"I don't care as long as they're healthy," she said definitively. She moved a little closer to them, lowering her voice. "Do you think anyone would notice if we slipped out now?"

"Are you tired? Do you need your rest?" asked Vander.

She shook her head. "I would like to go to bed, but I'm not a bit tired yet."

As soon as they grasped her meaning, they hustled her from the main chamber into their room in record time. She melted into their arms, experiencing the dizzying passion that always consumed her at their touch, and she knew she was exactly where she belonged.

Chapter 11

WHEN SHE AND VANDER and Virgo emerged from the wormhole the next morning, everything looked the same as she remembered, yet somehow different. The wormhole had brought them directly to the entrance of the base, and she still had access, so she pressed her hand to the biometric panel. She was afraid Freydon's changes to her body so she could grow gills and create a protective coating on her skin to survive underwater would alter her DNA enough that she wouldn't be recognized, but the door immediately opened.

She led them through the corridor, encountering various states of shock from the people around her. She smiled and nodded, but she didn't pause. She wanted to tell her parents first before anyone else.

It was early enough in the morning that they should still be in their quarters, but she only knocked vigorously on the door. Even if the system would let her in, she wasn't about to enter without permission. She was still traumatized from the time she'd done so as a teenager and learned that her parents were still very much in love and liked to show it to each other. She shuddered at the memory, but quickly pushed it aside as the door opened, and her father stood there. She threw herself against his blue form, hugging him as tears leaked from her eyes.

General DVS, or Davis as she and her mother and her siblings called him, wrapped his arms around her. "Where have you been? We were so worried."

"Eva?" Carrie's voice trembled as she said her name. With a cry, she rushed forward and wrapped her arms around Eva as well. Being hugged by her parents was the best feeling in the world, though she forced herself to pull back so she could explain.

"What happened to you?" asked Carrie, pushing strands of hair off Eva's face. "Why are you turning green?"

"And I have gills," said Eva with a shaky laugh as she pulled back her hair to show them.

Davis was glaring at Vander and Virgo. "Who are these men?"

"They're my mates. I've been on their planet, thanks to Freydon Rote."

Her parents both stiffened and looked at each other. Davis looked faintly annoyed, and Carrie just seemed surprised. "Freydon took you away without even a word to us?" She shook her head. "That doesn't sound like him."

Davis snorted. "Of course it does. He brought you here without much explanation, and he implied you were a weapon when I went to get you. The man's a manipulative little alien." The words were harsh, but there was still a strong tinge of affection in his tone.

"His manners are unorthodox, but..." Carrie trailed off. "I can't believe he didn't tell us he was taking you. Why didn't you say something or visit sooner?"

"He wouldn't let me have the ability to return until I decided I belonged with Vander and Virgo." As quickly as she could, she explained what had happened in the last month or so, not at all surprised when her father gave her mates the stink-eye.

"Are they taking care of you?" asked Davis.

"We'd die for her," said Vander.

"Absolutely, but Eva mostly takes care of herself. You raised her well," said Virgo with pride.

Davis nodded. "Perhaps Freydon knew what he was doing."

Carrie leaned forward to wrap her arm around Davis's waist. "He knew what he was doing for us. I have complete faith in him, though I'm a little miffed that he didn't tell us what was happening before he just took our daughter." She seemed to remember her manners then, as she held out her hand to first Vander and then Virgo. "If you love my daughter, and she loves you, that's good enough for me."

"There's more, Mom." Eva took her hand, squeezing lightly. "We're having a baby." She didn't share that it would most likely be twins or triplets, since she'd already given her parents enough to absorb for now.

Carrie let out a squeal, and Davis seemed to take it as though he'd been struck on the chin rather than heard good news. Eva could understand, since her father still regarded her as his little girl.

When Carrie and Davis could bear to share her, they joined the rest of the base in the mess hall. Eva hugged her brother Isaac (IZK) and her sister Ruby (RBY) before being swamped by her friends. It was a joyous reunion, but it started to wear on her, and she grew tired more quickly than she would have in the past. Perhaps it was just knowing that she was pregnant, but she'd felt more exhausted all day. If it was psychosomatic, it would resolve itself in roughly eight or nine months anyway.

As the day faded, she knew it was time for them to return to Senufo, so she pulled aside her family. "We need to get home, but I'll be back. I'll open the wormhole every few days and check in with you, because I don't want to lose touch with you. I love you all."

Her parents and siblings wrapped her in a hug, and Eva squeezed back as hard as she could before activating the wormhole. Vander and Virgo slipped through first, and she followed behind them as she waved to her family and friends back on Earth.

It had been wonderful to see them all again and to share what had happened, but she was relieved to be home. Her mates swept her off to bed, pampering and pleasuring her until she was exhausted, and her eyes wouldn't stay open. "I love you," she said to Vander, and then reached over to stroke Virgo's face too. "And I love you."

"We love you too," said Vander as Virgo nodded.

She felt them press tender kisses to her temples as she slipped into slumber, feeling cherished and protected.

Epilogue

ALMOST NINE MONTHS later

Eva gave birth with her mates beside her, and her mother in the corner of the room in their suite. Only her child turned out to be triplets. Three boys, and they all had the same shade of green skin, but with varying shades of hair. Leo had almost a cherry-red undertone to his black locks, while Viraz had a blue undertone, and the last born and smallest, Sero Freydon, had a deep lavender shade.

Eva half-hoped Freydon would pop in to see her babies, as he had done when she was born to Carrie, but there was no sign of him. He must've meant it when he said she wouldn't see him again, and it left her a little melancholy. He'd grown on her, and without him, none of this would've happened.

She soon forgot her sadness as Feltha placed Sero in her arms, while Vander held Viraz, and Virgo held Leo. She wasn't entirely certain how she was going to manage three babies, but she knew with two such wonderful husbands, who were clearly already doting fathers, they would manage just as the other Drakari did.

"Thank you," said Vander as he brushed his lips against her forehead.

She looked up at him. "I'm not sure you should thank me. It all just sort of happened, didn't it?"

"We did do our share to ensure this outcome," said Virgo with the lusty chuckle. He kept it low, since Carrie was approaching. "I love you," he whispered as her mother reached them.

Eva grinned at Carrie as she brushed her hand against each of her grandsons' foreheads. "They're absolutely beautiful, Eva. I can't wait for your father to be able to meet them."

Eva nodded, feeling a little sadness. Her father was too busy as the general of the enclave to be able to take a few days to stay with her during the birth. She and the babies would make a visit to Earth as soon as they were all up to it though. Right now, she was content to have her family around her, and she was excited to show her extended family her sons. How could she be anything but happy in that moment? It was just the first of many more ahead of her, and she said a silent thanks to Freydon that he'd probably never hear for deciding to meddle in her life and bring her so much joy.

More Titles

If you missed Carrie and DVS's story, you can read get it now:

ONE MOMENT, COMPLETELY human and modern-day Carrie Morgan is crocheting in her living room. The next second, a peach alien claiming to be a Celestial Mates agent transports her and her dog four hundred years into the future. He leaves her there to be discovered by her supposed fated mate—a blue-skinned cyborg general.

The sly agent failed to mention a few things, like the fact humans and cyborgs are at war with each other! She's certain Freydon Rote is crazy, but as she gets to know the cyborg general, she realizes maybe there's something to the claim that DVS84 is meant to be her mate. Passionate nights further convince her that perhaps she's in the right place at the right time to find her happy ending—if she survives all the challenges of her new environment.

A fun tidbit. Senufo is mentioned in this book, available at all retailers:

---

1. https://books2read.com/mttcg

AS THE SECOND-IN-COMMAND of Olympus Station, Captain Hadley Wells is usually too focused on her career to worry about romance. That changes with the arrival of Prince Nykal of Jroj, a planet that's recently joined the Coalition. Their attraction is immediate and fierce, but too many rules separate them to let them have more than one stolen night. The night is amazing, but has far-reaching consequences. Add in the ambassador determined to keep Nykal from her by any means, and it's a complicated mess that needs a solution before the secret she carries is visible to all.

You can find a complete list of my books on my website: http://kittunstall.com

---

2. https://books2read.com/u/bzvPZj

About Aurelia

AURELIA SKYE IS THE pen name *USA Today* bestselling author Kit Tunstall uses when writing science fiction romance. It's simply a way to separate the myriad types of stories she writes so readers know what to expect with each "author."

If you enjoyed this story and would like to receive notifications of new releases or access bonus chapters for your favorite books, please join my Mailing List[1]**. You'll also receive free books just for joining. If you prefer to receive notifications for just one, or a few, of my pen names, you'll have the option to select which lists to subscribe to at signup.**

---

1. http://kittunstall.com/newsletter/

Did you love *Destined For The Drakari Warlords*? Then you should read *Cybernetic Hearts: Complete Series*[2] by Aurelia Skye!

Celestial Mates Agent Freydon Rote sets in motion four mate pairings in the Cybernetic Hearts series. It all begins when he brings modern-day human Carrie four centuries into the future, where she finds a ravaged planet and a war between humans and cyborgs—and also the love of her life in the cyborg general, DVS84. Their match is the catalyst for cyborgs JSN42, MX, and RVN to find their human mates while finding a way to end the war between the cyborgs and humans while fighting their mutual enemy, the synths.

The complete collection includes:

"Mated To The Cyborg General"

"Claimed By The Cyborg Commander"

---

2. https://books2read.com/u/b6Mr9W

3. https://books2read.com/u/b6Mr9W

"Fated For the Cyborg Officer"
"Meant For The Cyborg Captain"
"Baby For The Cyborg General"

Also by Aurelia Skye

Alien Baby Pact
Baby For The Brundle Commander
Baby For The Grimlock General
Baby For The Palantir Chief
Baby For The Alphan Captain

Celestial Mates
Wrong Place, Right Mate
Destined For The Drakari Warlords

Cybernetic Hearts
Mated To The Cyborg General
Claimed By The Cyborg Commander
Fated For The Cyborg Officer
Meant For The Cyborg Captain
Baby For The Cyborg General
Cybernetic Hearts: Complete Series

Hell Virus
Catching Hell
Surviving Hell
Bleeding Hell
Raising Hell
Sharing Hell

Howls Romance
The Jaguar Alpha's Forbidden Lover

Northstar Shifters
Northstar Heir's Scarred Mate

Olympus Station
Station Commander's Surrogate
Alien Prince's Secret Baby
Security Agent's Alien Bartender
Olympus Station Compilation

SpicyShorts
Music In My Heart
Kilted Tentacle Monster: A Search for True Love

Sweet Escapes
Hook & Wendy

Three Crones Inn
Vastly Inn-proved
Ghastly Intentions
Ghostly Inn-heritance
Three Crones Inn Compilation

True North
True North #1: Death & Deception
True North #2: Rescued & Revelations
True North #3: Fire & Ice
True North #4: Enemies & Lovers
True North #5: Truth & Tiranog
True North #6: Fight & Flight
True North #7: Love & Loss

Wounded Warriors
Relentless
Marked
Justice
Wounded Warriors Collection
Hunted

Standalone
Reluctant Companion
Princess By Mistake
Fire Lord's Assistant
True North
Dragon Laird's Witch
Alien General's Rebel Consort
Tempted By Demons
Enemy Combatant
Grotesquerie
Mistaken Bounty

www.ingramcontent.com/pod-product-compliance
Lightning Source LLC
Chambersburg PA
CBHW050545160726
48003CB00002B/764